Paula Danziger has no  them. She lives in Her hobbies are playing video games ene globes of different pla

If you meet someone w blonde or brown hair, wearing lots of jewe saying 'Are we there yet?' or 'Yuk, spinach!', she could just be Paula Danziger!

Paula Danziger

EVERYONE ELSE'S PARENTS SAID YES!

AND

MAKE LIKE A TREE AND LEAVE

PIPER

PAN MACMILLAN

CHILDREN'S BOOKS

Everyone Else's Parents Said Yes!
first published in Great Britain 1989 by
William Heinemann Ltd.
Piper edition published 1990 by
Pan Books Ltd., Cavaye Place, London SW10 9PG
in association with Heinemann
© Paula Danziger 1989

Make Like a Tree and Leave
First published in the United States of America 1990 by
Delacorte Press, New York
Piper edition published in Great Britain 1991 by
Pan Macmillan Children's Books
A division of Pan Macmillan Ltd.,
Cavaye Place, London SW10 9PG
© Paula Danziger 1990

This double edition published in
1993 by Pan Macmillan Children's
Books, Cavaye Place, London SW10 9PG
and Basingstoke

ISBN: 330 33487 5

Printed and bound in Great Britain by
Cox & Wyman Ltd, Reading, Berkshire

EVERYONE
ELSE'S PARENTS
SAID YES!

ACKNOWLEDGEMENTS

Patricia Reilly Giff: for support and 'noodging'
The Danzigers: Barry, Annette, Sam, Carrie, Ben and Josh
The Stantons: Fank, David, Paul and Brian
*The children all over the country who have shared their
ideas, experiences and suggestions*

To
*Fran and Jules Davids,
with a lifetime
of love*

EVERYONE ELSE'S PARENTS SAID YES!

CHAPTER 1

'Mom. You know there are only five more days, fifteen hours and thirty-two minutes until my birthday party.' Matthew enters the kitchen holding a computer printout.

Matthew Martin can be very organised and accurate when he wants to be, and he wants to be. Since he's the youngest person in his sixth grade class, birthdays really count.

'I know, honey. One hour ago, you came in here and told me that there were only five more days, *sixteen* hours and thirty-two minutes until your birthday party.' Mrs Martin can also be very organised and accurate, even while she is busy following the recipe for zucchini carob chip bread.

'Listen to him. You'd think that no one ever had an eleventh birthday before.' Amanda Martin applies polish to her very bitten down nails and wrinkles her nose at her brother. 'I didn't make a big fuss about it two years ago when I had my eleventh birthday. You're such a big baby.'

'Two years ago, you *did* make a big fuss about it.'

Mrs Martin grins, reminding her. 'Nothing would do but to take twelve girls to *ADORNABLE YOU*, the store where you make things to decorate yourself.'

Matthew offers, 'I'll get the picture out of the scrapbook to prove it. You and those goofy girls wearing . . .' Pausing, he puts his hand on his hip and acts like a model. 'All those silly feather things and ugly sparkly jewellery. Goofy, goofy girls. Yuck.'

'Shut up, runt.' Amanda glares at him.

'I'm not a runt. Just a little short for my age. Daddy says he was like that too, and now look at how tall he is!' Matthew shouts at her. 'And look at you, runt chest, who do you think you are?'

Mrs Martin sighs. 'Amanda, stop calling your brother a runt and Matthew, don't refer to your sister's chest as a runt chest. In fact, don't refer to your sister's chest at all.'   Amanda and Matthew can tell that their mother is trying not to grin.

Amanda stands up and yells, 'It's not funny! He's disgusting. I hate him. And you make it worse by laughing at what he says. Why did he ever have to be born? Why did I?'

'She always acts like the big shot she isn't.' Matthew sticks his tongue out at her.

Amanda stomps out of the room.

Mrs Martin puts her hand on her head, leaving batter on her forehead. 'Children. I should have got goldfish as pets instead.'

'Then you could have had a pool party for the

goldfishes' birthday.' Matthew licks the cake beaters.

Wiping the batter off her forehead, Mrs Martin says, 'Very funny. Now Matthew, I want you to stop teasing your sister so much. She's just entering adolescence, actually stomping her way into it, and it's not going to be an easy time for her. Not for her . . . not for me . . . not for any of us, I have a feeling.'

'I was born to drive her nuts,' Matthew informs her. 'And we both know that's not going to be a long trip.'

'Matthew.' His mother has a way of saying the name so that it takes forever and means stop being a wise guy.

'Oh, okay, Mom.' Matthew puts down the cake beaters. 'Now, about the party: you said I should think about it. Well, I've decided. I want a sleep-over in the garden.'

'Okay. Remember, your father and I work hard and we need your help with the party.' Mrs Martin smiles.

'Right.' Matthew shows her the computer print-out in his hands. 'Don't worry. I've got everything under control. Here are the lists.'

Mrs Martin pours the batter into a pan, puts the pan into the oven, sets the timer, washes and dries her hands, and finally sits down to look over Matthew's lists.

THE KIDS

BILLY KELLERMAN
TYLER WHITE
JOSHUA JACKSON
BRIAN BRUNO
DAVID COHEN
PATRICK RYAN
MARK ELLISON
PABLO MARTINEZ

THE FOOD

HOT DOGS
HAMBURGERS
POTATO CHIPS
SODA
CAKE
ICE CREAM
ALL THE JUNK FOOD
IN THE WORLD

THINGS TO DO

GET PRESENTS

OPEN PRESENTS

HAVE COMPUTER NINTENDO TOURNAMENTS

GIVE OUT PRIZES TO TOURNAMENT WINNERS

EAT

ALL OF US MAKE FUN OF AMANDA AT ONCE

TELL JOKES

GIVE OUT PRIZES FOR BEST JOKES

GO TO SLEEP

WAKE UP

EAT

ALL OF US MAKE FUN OF HOW AMANDA
LOOKS IN THE MORNING

EVERYONE GOES HOME

PLAY WITH MY PRESENTS

'I think that you are going to have to re-examine your lists.' Matthew's mother smiles. 'The guest list is fine but there are a few items in the other lists that will have to go.'

'Okay, so we won't go to sleep.' Matthew grins at her.

'That's not it, kiddo.' She pats him on the head. 'You will leave your sister out of this.'

'That's all I ever want to do: leave my sister out of everything, my life, the house . . .' Matthew sticks his fingers into the left over zucchini batter and then licks them.

'Matthew.'

'Oh, okay. I'll take all of the stuff about her off the lists. Then will everything else be okay?'

Another 'Matthew.'

'Yes.' He grins, knowing what she's going to say.

'I really feel that you should reconsider all that awful junk food on your list and make some healthy substitutions — carob candy, fruit bars, things like that.'

'Come on, Mom. Everyone else's parents let them eat junk food.'

Mrs Martin sighs. 'Matthew Martin. How many times must I tell you that we're not everyone else's parents. If everyone else's parents let them jump off the roof, should we let *you* jump off the roof?'

'It's just a little junk food, not nuclear destruction,' Matthew pleads.

'I'm not sure that there's much difference between eating junk food and nuclear destruction.'

Mrs Martin shakes her head.

Matthew sometimes wishes that his mother were more like his best friend Joshua Jackson's mother, who says things like, 'Isn't Granola a Latin American country?' and 'Tofu, isn't that the crud under your toenails?'

'Mom, please. Look, the guys will hate me if we serve the stuff you like. They call *that* stuff junk food, and even Dad likes junk food . . . and anyway, everyone else's . . .' Matthew stops himself from repeating his favourite phrase.

Mrs Martin sighs again. 'This is against my better judgement, but all right. You may have *some* junk food at your party. It's a losing battle with you sometimes, but I'm telling you right now. I'm going to make a very healthy cake.'

'Oh, okay.' Matthew tries to look sad, like he's giving in, but deep down inside he feels like he's won the Super Bowl prize for Handling Mothers. He's actually got his mother to agree to some junk food!

It was going to be a great party, no doubt about it.

CHAPTER 2

'Hey, want to swap desserts?' Matthew stares at the contents of Joshua Jackson's lunch box.

'Are you kidding? Your mom makes you eat healthy junk.'

Joshua takes out a packet of three cupcakes, which are filled with cream and covered with marshmallow and coconut icing.

'Please, I'll be your best friend if you share those with me.' Matthew holds back a drool.

'You already are my best friend.' Joshua starts taking the cellophane off the cupcakes.

'Ummm. Look at this.' Matthew holds up his dessert.

'What is it?' Joshua makes a face.

'Wholewheat fruit slices. Yummy. I'd be willing to give up four of them, all four of them, for just one of your three cupcakes. What a deal!' Matthew holds up the packet as if he's holding up a trophy.

'No deal.' Joshua licks the top of one of the cupcakes and then takes a bite out of it.

'I'll be your best *best* friend,' Matthew pleads.

'You said that last week. What was that mess I swapped a cupcake for?'

'Cottage Cheese Yoghurt Cake,' Matthew reminds him. 'Oh, Joshua. This is better. Come on. Please. I can't help it if my mother makes me eat this stuff.'

Joshua looks at his remaining two cupcakes and then at his best friend. 'Here's the deal. I give you the cupcake. You don't give me the fruit slices.'

'Fair deal.' Matthew reaches for a cupcake.

'Not yet.' Joshua stops Matthew's hand in mid-grab. 'You have to help me learn how to play Defender Dragons better.'

Defender Dragons. Matthew's best computer game, the one where he racks up the highest scores of anyone in the class, of anyone in the entire school.

Matthew looks at his friend, then at the cupcake, and back to his friend. The cupcake. The friend. 'All right, not all of my manoeuvres, but enough to get you to the next level. How about that?'

'It's a deal.' Joshua hands over a cupcake and thinks that with the kind of stuff Matthew's mother cooks, he's going to be able to learn how to get to all of the levels.

As Matthew puts the cupcake into his mouth, he tries to eat it slowly, tasting every little bit, licking the icing, eating the cake, saving the cream centre until the end.

It's too late. Something in Matthew acts like a

vacuum cleaner, sucking up the cupcake in what seems like seconds.

Looking down at the wholewheat fruit slices, Matthew thinks of how his parents are always telling him not to waste food, to think of the poor starving people in the world.

Mr Farley, the head lunchroom monitor, goes up to the microphone, taps it and yells into it. *'All right, you kids!* It's time to go out to the playground. Don't forget the rules. Make sure all litter is put in the bins, go out quietly, no pushing or shoving and if anyone has spilled milk or food, notify us immediately so that no one gets hurt.'

Mr Farley has been very worried about spilling since the time he rushed over to stop a fight between two sixth grade boys and he slipped on milk and banana.

He broke his foot and used crutches for a long time to walk and once to separate the same two sixth grade boys who were fighting again.

Everyone rushes out.

Mr Farley steps back.

Matthew gets into line to throw out his rubbish.

Lizzie Doran is in front of him.

Stepping on the back of her sneakers, he says, 'Ooops, so sorry.'

She turns round. 'I know you're not sorry. Matthew Martin, you are so immature.'

'Thank you.' Matthew loves to annoy Lizzie.

'You're not welcome.' She turns her back and ignores him.

Matthew smiles.

School gets boring sometimes, he thinks. It's fun to do stuff like this.

Matthew throws out his rubbish, holding on to his dessert which he places under a tree outside thinking that maybe some poor starving birds would like to eat it.

As he looks down at the wholewheat fruit slices, he thinks that the birds won't like it either, that they would prefer worms, that he would probably prefer worms if he were a bird.

'Keepaway! Sixth grade boys over here to play Keepaway,' Brian Bruno is yelling.

Joshua and Matthew run over to where Brian is standing with the ball and start running from it as fast as they can.

Matthew is beaned by Tyler White.

As Matthew stands on the sidelines and watches, he is glad that Tyler White is no good at Defender Dragons.

Looking round the playground, Matthew checks on what everyone is doing. The six graders are hogging all the best spaces, like they always do. At Elizabeth Englebert Elementary, where the cheer 'Go E.E.E.' sounds like pigs squealing, the sixth graders get dibs on practically everything.

Matthew has waited a long time for his class to reach the sixth grade. The next big event for him will be becoming a teenager.

Matthew thinks about his approaching birthday and how he's getting closer.

Looking at the sixth grade girls who are also playing Keepaway but at the other side of the playground, Matthew thinks about how it was back in the old days at E.E.E. when they all played together, not just in gym class.

Something had changed and now it was all different.

Matthew remembers how he spent the first few weeks getting used to the school's new computer graphics program and teaching all the boys how to make fancy signs for their doors that said ALL GIRLS, KEEP OUT. THIS MEANS YOU.

It amazed Matthew that not all of the boys were interested in making that sign, that some of them even wanted to make others — especially Patrick Ryan, who made one that said ALL GIRLS, ENTER. THIS MEANS YOU.

Mark Ellison is out next, yelling, 'Not fair!'

Mark Ellison always thinks it isn't fair when he loses.

Then Patrick Ryan is out. He walks away making jokes as if he doesn't care, but he does. Patrick Ryan plays to win.

Soon it is down to Joshua against Tyler White.

Tyler throws the ball at Joshua's head, but Joshua ducks, grabs the ball and throws it at Tyler, hitting him on the rear end.

Everyone cheers and gives high fives to Joshua.

Heads you lose, tails you win, thinks Matthew as the bell rings, signalling back-to-class time.

Usually Matthew hates that bell, but not today.

Today he's going to ask Mrs Stanton for time to do his party invitations using the new computer graphics program.

He can hardly wait.

CHAPTER 3

'We sent out two gorillas in tutus, one six-foot tall pink singing chicken, four tap dancing birthday cakes, a teddy bear on roller skates and a grandmother who delivers chicken soup.' Mrs Martin hands the plate of broccoli to Mr Martin. 'And that was just the early part of today.'

Mr Martin is interested in his wife's new job at the place that sends out people in costumes to deliver singing telegrams, gifts, balloonograms and other surprises for special occasions. 'What about later in the day?'

'It was a disaster. There were only two major jobs — a birthday party for a six-year-old and a fiftieth wedding anniversary. Mickey Mouse and Minnie Mouse were supposed to tap dance a birthday song to the kid and a man in a tuxedo was supposed to deliver a dozen roses to the couple. Did that happen? No. It did not.'

Waiting for a minute to build up the suspense, Mrs Martin shrugs.

Matthew, trying to find a good place to hide the

broccoli, asks, 'What happened?'

'Mrs Grimbell, the owner, made a mistake and confused the orders. She seems a little distracted. Anyway, the guy in the tuxedo delivered the roses to the boy who kept saying, 'Where are my helium balloons? I wanted us to inhale them and make our voices change,' and the couple could not quite believe that there, in their own living room, were Mickey and Minnie tap dancing "Happy Anniversary to You," and throwing confetti all over the place.'

'What did the old folks say?' Mathew chops up his broccoli and puts it under the rim of his plate.

'The woman kept saying, "Look at this mess. Are you planning to vacuum it up?" and the husband said, "Helium balloons. Great. We can inhale them and listen to our voices."' Mrs Martin laughs.

'It sounds much more exciting than my day,' Mr Martin says. 'Want to swap? I'll take your job and you can be a lawyer.'

'Nope.' Mrs Martin shakes her head. 'I like what I'm doing. However, maybe you can help out. There's a chance that tomorrow I will be one person short. Would you be willing to put on a gorilla suit and go to an engagement party, wearing a sign that says, *Melvin Goes Ape Over Gina*?'

'I'd love to.' Mr Martin nods. 'And then I can wear the gorilla suit in court. That way the people who believe that there's a lot of *monkey business* going on in court will think that they have proof.'

'Daddy. Don't. I'd die if anyone saw you dressed

as a gorilla,' Amanda whines. 'And Mom, why can't you get a normal job like other mothers? You do this just to embarrass me. Everyone's asking if you do strip grams.'

'Not me personally.' Mrs Martin acts horrified. 'And Amanda, your father and I are just kidding around. He's not going to get dressed in costumes.'

'Shucks.' Mr Martin looks sad. 'You have all the fun. You can dress up in all these costumes.'

'Only if it's an emergency. That's not my regular job,' Mrs Martin reminds them.

'Mom. Promise you won't wear costumes. I would die!' Amanda begs and threatens.

Mrs Martin shrugs. 'A woman's got to do what a woman's got to do.'

Deciding to change the subject, Mrs Martin holds up the plate.

'Anyone want seconds of the tuna tofu casserole?'

'No thanks.' Matthew shakes his head, waves the plate away and wonders what Joshua is eating tonight.

'No thanks, honey.' Mr Martin looks down at his half full plate and remembers the great meal he had at lunch. 'So, kids, how was your day?'

'Great.'

'Terrible.'

Both responses come out at the same time.

'Which of you would like to go first?' Mr Martin asks.

'He might as well, since his day was so wonderful

and mine wasn't.' Amanda bites her nails.

'Honey, stop biting your nails.' Mrs Martin reaches for Amanda's hand.

Amanda pulls her hand away.

Matthew decides to ignore Amanda and speak. 'Mrs Stanton gave me permission to work on my party invitations using the new program, and I've decided what to put in the goody bag, and everyone I'm inviting is going to be able to come to the sleepover.'

'What do you need the invitations for, then?' Amanda asks.

Matthew continues to ignore Amanda. 'And I've got a great idea for the design of the invitation and the graphics and the colours.'

'I really should upgrade our machine.' Mr Martin thinks out loud.

Amanda jabs at her tuna tofu. 'Doesn't anyone care about my day? All he's talking about is making up invitations for the party to send to people who already know about it and have already said that they're coming. How dumb can you get?'

'Amanda.' Mrs Martin makes the name sound five times as long.

'Well, it's true. And here I sit with my life in a shambles, and it's all your fault.' Amanda's lower lip moves forward.

'Why is it our fault?' Mr Martin asks.

'Today, Bobby Fenton called me *four eyes*.'

Well, she is, Matthew thinks, annoyed at being interrupted. The four F's: — Four Eyed, Flat, Funny

Looking, and Fingernail-Stubbed.

He bites his lip to keep from saying it out loud. No reason to take a chance on getting grounded just before his party.

Amanda starts to cry. 'It's all your fault. If only you'd let me get contact lenses. . .'

'No. We've been through this already. Dr Sugarman says to wait a little bit longer. By next year, you can get them.'

'Next year,' Amanda sighs. 'Everyone else's parents let them get contact lenses this year.'

Not true, Matthew thinks, knowing at least six of her classmates who wear glasses.

'We're not everyone else's parents.' Her mother says. 'We're your parents and we say that you must wait for the lenses until the doctor thinks it's right.'

'A year.' Amanda makes a face. 'Well, at least let me have plastic surgery, then.'

'What!' Her parents yell at the same time.

'For my ears. One is lower than the other and my glasses are crooked. If my ears were even, the glasses wouldn't be tilted.'

Everyone looks at Amanda's face.

Everyone thinks her glasses look perfectly fine.

Mr and Mrs Martin think her face looks perfectly fine.

Matthew thinks she should have plastic surgery on her entire face.

'Amanda. Be reasonable. Dr Sugarman said that there was a slight difference in your ears, that many people have that problem and that all it takes is to adjust the glasses a little. He did that. There's no problem. You are very pretty.' her father says.

'You're my father. You have to say that.' A tear rolls down Amanda's face.

Matthew cannot understand what she's making such a big deal about and hopes that he doesn't turn weird when he becomes a teenager.

He also thinks about how long it will be before she goes away to college and he has the house and his parents to himself. Too long. Not soon enough.

Tomorrow wouldn't be soon enough, let alone five years.

While Amanda continues, Matthew tunes out and thinks about the contents of the goody bag that each person at the party will get — M&Ms, a box of raisins, Sweet Tarts, wax teeth with fangs, a packet of baseball cards with bubble gum, and one of those liquorice rolls with a sweet centre. He's happy with the choices — junk food with one healthy thing, the raisins, to make his mother a little happier. To make himself a little happier, he would have added about eight other kinds of sweets, but his parents and the budget that they gave him wouldn't allow it.

He tunes back in to what's happening.

Amanda is still talking. 'And it's all your fault that I have to wear glasses. If you two didn't have bad eyes, I wouldn't.'

Matthew thinks, maybe she should blame it on their grandparents. They had to wear glasses, too. Maybe she should blame it on the dinosaurs. They probably caused cavemen to squint from looking up at them. Then the cavemen needed glasses and it was passed on to future generations.

Amanda doesn't give up. 'And it's not fair. Look at that little twerp. He doesn't have to wear glasses.'

'That's because they like me better than they like you,' Matthew teases. 'And my ears aren't even lop-sided.'

Matthew has trouble stopping once he starts. 'And I'm not ugly, and dumb, and acting like a turkey.'

Amanda stands up. 'You repulsive little runt.'

'Enough!' Mrs Martin yells.

'To your rooms. Both of you,' Mr Martin orders.

'It's not my fault!' Amanda and Matthew yell at the same time.

'Well, it's definitely not our fault,' their father says. 'I want you to go to your rooms and think about what you've done.'

Both kids go off to their rooms, mumbling, 'It's not fair. It's not my fault.'

Matthew goes to his room and thinks about what he's done. Nothing.

It's Amanda's fault.

It always is.

Someday, he thinks, *some* day, I'm going to get even.

CHAPTER 4

Roses are red,
Violets are perkle.
Amanda Martin is a four-eyed jerkle.

'Matthew. That's not very nice.' Mrs Stanton looks over his shoulder. 'And I don't think that you've really followed the assignment.'

'Why not?' Matthew, with an ink mark on his nose, looks up at her. 'You said that we should make up a greeting card using words and numbers. Well, I did.'

'That's not a very nice greeting,' Mrs Stanton tells him.

'It's for my sister. She's not a very nice person so she doesn't deserve a very nice greeting card. The only greeting she ever gives me is, "Get out of my way, nerd face."'

'Matthew. When your sister was in my class, she was very nice. I know that brothers and sisters don't always get along.' Mrs Stanton speaks softly. 'But your sister is really very nice. Some day, I'm sure you will realise it.'

Matthew says, 'I'm never going to like my sister. She's turned into a monster. We're never going to get along, ever. Not now. Not when we're ninety.'

'Well, I hope that you aren't always going to feel that way, and Matthew, you really shouldn't call people names. It's not right to call someone four-eyes.'

Matthew realises that Mrs Stanton is wearing glasses.

He's not sure what to say.

She continues, 'And you shouldn't call her a jerk.'

He knows what to say about that. 'I didn't. I

called her a jerkle. That's a word that I made up. It means "dear, sweet, wonderful sister."'

He can tell by the look on Mrs Stanton's face that she doesn't believe him.

He wouldn't believe himself either if he were the teacher.

Mrs Stanton sighs. 'Start again, Matthew. Throw that card away and start over.'

Matthew pleads, 'Do I have to?'

'Yes.' Mrs Stanton means business.

'I'll do a card to my mother and I'll throw this one away later.' He promises, knowing that there is no way that he wants to throw out the card to Amanda.

'It's your choice, Matthew. Throw that card away now and be able to use the computer later for your invitations or hold on to the card and not be able to use the computer later for your invitations.'

'Ah.' Matthew knows when he's beaten. 'I'll throw the card out now.'

'Good boy.' Mrs Stanton says.

Matthew goes up to the waste paper basket, puts the card in and thinks about how he's going to make another card when he gets home.

Jill Hudson calls out 'Oh. Oh. Oh!' She keeps waving her hand.

Jill Hudson finds it impossible to just hold up her hand and wait until she gets called on by a teacher. She has had this habit since kindergarten.

'Yes, Jill.' Mrs Stanton calls on her.

'Can I make an announcement to the class? Oh, Oh, Oh. It's very important.' Jill is practically jumping out of her chair.

'Very important?' Mrs Stanton doesn't sound so sure.

'Oh. Oh. *IT IS! IT IS!*'

'All right.' Mrs Stanton looks like she's not too sure that she's making the right decision.

Jill announces, 'I've decided that my name is very boring.'

'So are you!' Brian calls out and then pretends to yawn.

All of the boys start pretending to yawn.

Jill ignores them. 'Everyone else has nice names, like Cathy, who can also be called Cath, or Catherine. Lizzie can be Liz or Elizabeth. Ryma, whose mother promised to name her after her grandmother Mary, but made the name nice and different. Lisa Levine, whose names go well together. Vanessa, Jessica, Zoe and Chloe, who have beautiful names if people don't make them sound like they rhyme with toe.' Jill stands up at her desk. 'You know, if they make them rhyme with Joey —'

'Jill, please get to the point.' Mrs Stanton is grinning and shaking her head.

'I am. I am. Katie can be Kate or Katherine or Kath, and Sarah's name is just so pretty.'

'The point, Jill. You've named all of the girls in the class so get to the point.'

Mrs Stanton looks up at the clock on the wall. 'It's almost time for break.'

Jill gets to the point.

Jill is not the kind of person who likes to be late for break.

'I've decided to make my name more exciting. I can't change it to Jilly because the dumb boys will make it rhyme with Silly.'

'And Pilly and Dilly,' Tyler calls out.

'Billy and Jilly sitting in a tree.

K — I — S — S — I — N — G.'

'Shut up, Tyler!' Billy Kellerman yells out. 'I'm going to get you for that.'

'Children.' Mrs Stanton uses her 'very teacher' tone.

Jill ignores all the fuss. 'So I've decided that from now on my name will be spelt Jil!, with an explanation point at the end to make it more exciting.'

'Ex*clam*ation point,' Mrs Stanton grins.

'Whatever.' Jill, now Jil!, goes on, 'And when you say my name make it very dramatic, because that's what the explanat — because that's what that mark means.'

'Oh! Oh! Oh!' Pablo waves his hand, doing a Jil! imitation.

'Mrs Stanton, I think that it should be Jil? with a question mark instead. To show that it isn't easy to understand how Jil? got so weird.'

The bell rings for break.

Mrs Stanton excuses the class.

The students, except for Matthew, rush outside.

Matthew sits down at the computer, prepares a new disc, and begins.

It's going to be the best invitation ever.

31

CHAPTER 5

Computers.

Cakes.

Stars with elevens in them.

A tent.

All the important information.

It had taken Matthew the entire break and lunch period to finish, but it was worth it.

Everyone would know that Matthew Martin was the best in computer design.

He did the work himself.

No program for him.

He was the best.

No one could beat him at computer.

David Cohen was better at remembering the planets and elements.

Katie Delaney always won the spelling bees. In fact, practically everyone in the class was a better speller than Matthew.

Joshua and Tyler were great athletes.

Brian Bruno was already a brown belt in karate.

Best artist was Mark Ellison.

**BIRTHDAY PARTY
SLEEP-OVER
MATTHEW MARTIN**

114 Third St.
Califon, N.J.

Day: This Friday
Time: 7:00 pm to Sat. 11am
Bring Sleeping Bag & Pillow
Date: 21st - 22nd

All the girls thought that Patrick Ryan was 'the cutest'.

Matthew doesn't care about cute. He doesn't think much about what he looks like. He knows that he has straight brown hair that never looks combed even when it is, because Amanda is always saying things like 'Doofus. You should use hair conditioner on that mess.' Amanda also says, 'Your eyes look like they could use a pooper scooper.' It's not the brown eyes that bother Matthew, but the freckles drive him nuts. His grandmother always pinches his cheeks and says, 'My darling little freckle face.' Matthew knows that he doesn't look like Frankenstein, Dracula or Freddy from Nightmare on Elm Street. What he doesn't know is what makes a girl think that someone's cute and actually he doesn't care that he doesn't know.

What he does care about is computers and no one could ever say that Matthew Martin wasn't the best at computer, especially after they see the invitations.

Matthew continues work on the invitations, adding little details, while the rest of the class comes running in.

'Hey, Matthew. You missed it. I got six baskets.' Joshua pretends to still be dribbling the ball.

'Great.' Matthew doesn't look up.

'Matthew. It was really fantastic. You should have been there.' Joshua tries to get his friend's attention.

Matthew still doesn't look up.

'That's it.' Joshua is getting annoyed. 'Stop with that stupid machine already. *Or else*.'

Looking up, Matthew sees that Joshua is holding on to the computer cord.

'Don't fool around with that!' Matthew yells.

In the background, he can hear Tyler singing 'Billy and Jilly sitting in a tree.'

'Stop that!' Billy yells, 'or you're going to be sorry — very sorry.'

Before Joshua can put down the computer cord, Billy pushes Tyler, who bumps into Joshua, who accidentally pulls the plug out of the extension.

It's all over for the invitation, which Matthew had not yet stored.

Matthew stares at the now darkened computer monitor.

Joshua comes over and looks at the screen. 'I'm sorry. I didn't mean to. It was an accident.'

The rest of the class comes into the room.

Mrs Stanton, who comes in last, takes one look at the room and rushes up to pull Billy off Tyler, who is lying face down on the floor.

'It was an accident. I slipped.' Billy tries to look innocent.

'Sit down.' Mrs Stanton points to a chair.

'Are you all right?' She helps Tyler get up and hands him a tissue for his bloody nose.

'Gross.' Chloe looks at the blood coming down Tyler's face.

Matthew continues to stare at the darkened monitor.

'Everyone sit down while I take care of this,' Mrs Stanton says.

'I'm sorry,' Joshua repeats, tugging on Matthew's sweatshirt. 'Come on. Say something.'

Matthew looks at the screen where four minutes earlier had been something that he had been planning for weeks and had worked on for most of the day, the free time part of the day.

It was all gone.

'Joshua. Go to your seat.' Mrs Stanton calls out. 'Now.'

'Say something,' Joshua says, before heading for his seat. 'Say something.'

Matthew glares at him and whispers, 'I hate you. I don't want you to come to my party. I don't want you to be my friend.'

'Well, if you feel that way about it, who cares. You act so dumb sometimes.' Joshua turns and goes to his seat.

'Matthew. Back to your seat too. You can finish that invitation later.' Mrs Stanton walks with Tyler to the door. 'Tyler, go to the nurse and then I want you to go to the principal's office and explain what happened.'

Billy Kellerman is smiling because Tyler has to go to the principal.

'You may go there right now, William Kellerman,' Mrs Stanton says.

Billy Kellerman stops smiling and gets up.

Matthew Martin is sitting at his desk and feeling rotten.

CHAPTER 6

Today has to be one of the worst days of Matthew's life.

Three whole days without speaking to Joshua . . . and today Joshua was really disgusting.

Joshua Jackson, his best friend — no, his ex-best friend — brought in bags and boxes of junk food for everyone, everyone except his best friend, his ex-best friend, Matthew Martin.

It must have cost him two months' allowance. There were jujubes, sugar babies, gum drops, chocolate necco wafers, cheetos, sour cream and onion ruffle potato crisps, circus peanuts, snickers, gummy bears, worms and dinosaurs, Reeses peanut butter cups and M&Ms, plain and peanut. It was torture.

Passing the junk out at lunch to all of the sixth graders, except for his ex-best friend, Joshua ignored Matthew except to say, 'Enjoying your rice cakes with sugar-free jam, turkey?'

'If you want more,' Joshua informed everyone, 'you better not give any to Matthew.'

It was terrible.

Lizzie Doran refused to take any because it was mean, what Joshua was doing to Matthew, even though it was true that Matthew sometimes drove her nuts.

Matthew decided that Lizzie Doran was okay and that he would never again do things to bug her.

Brian Bruno sneaked one brown M&M to Matthew.

Then at Keepaway, Matthew was not only the first person out, but he was out because he got slammed by Joshua.

Before, Joshua had never aimed for Matthew. It was always someone else who had got him out.

In school, Matthew noticed that Joshua was having trouble with one of the computer programs.

When Joshua said, 'Could someone give me a hand with this?' Matthew pretended to be engrossed in a maths problem.

After school, the time when the two boys usually hung out together, both went home alone, even though they lived down the street from each other.

Both acted as if it didn't matter, as if they were invisible to each other.

Now Matthew was home and there was more trouble.

'Kids. Your mother has to work late and I don't want to miss bowling tonight. It's the first round of the tournament,' Mr Martin tells his children.

Matthew is rummaging through the refrigerator, hoping that one of the carrot sticks has magically turned into a lemon meringue pie.

Amanda is in the kitchen only because she has been called downstairs for this discussion.

Most of the time, she stays in her room, pouting about being contact lens-less, about not being able to have plastic surgery on her ears and about not being able to have a private phone in her room.

Mr Martin continues, 'Now, listen. I've tried to get a baby sitter.'

'I don't need one,' Amanda informs him. 'Kids my age are baby sitting already.'

'That's what I want to talk to you about,' Mr Martin says. 'I want you to babysit for us today.'

'I'm not a baby. I don't need a sitter!' Matthew yells. 'And definitely not *her*.'

'Are you going to pay me?' Amanda is thinking about the possibility of saving up to have her own private phone installed.

'Are you going to pay *me*?' Matthew is thinking about how he deserves combat pay for putting up with his sister.

Mr Martin shakes his head. 'You two are impossible. You should be happy to help out, to be part of the family. The only reason for a babysitter is that your mother and I won't be home until very late and that we don't think it's safe to leave the two of you at home alone, without a referee. However, we can't seem to locate one for tonight. They are probably all officiating at wrestling matches and hockey games instead of realising that we would need them to watch our children.'

'That's because you won't leave junk food for

39

them, the babysitters, I mean. They're all sick of the stuff in our refrigerator,' Amanda informs them.

Matthew is not surprised by this piece of information.

However, his father is. 'Honey, that's not true. We've always tipped very well and no one has ever complained.'

'It's in the unwritten babysitters' code not to complain to the parents. But it is true. I know it is. There's a kid in my class, Sharlene, and her older sister, Darlene, babysits a lot. Darlene told Sharlene that there's a list that babysitters share with each other grading all of their jobs. In the food category, we got a G.'

'What's a G?' Mr Martin is getting a headache.

'It's like the school grades, where we get A, B, C, D, or F. We didn't even rate an F. We were below Failure.' Amanda sighs. 'It's so hard being part of this family.'

Standing up, Mr Martin holds up his hands to signal *stop*. 'I've got to get going. Now I want you to be in charge, Amanda. I will pay you.'

'Not fair.' Matthew yells. 'I'm in sixth grade. You treat me like such a baby. No one else's parents get a baby sitter.'

'Be good and I'll pay you too.' Mr Martin offers. 'I can't believe it. I'm offering my children bribes to act like human beings. It's against everything I believe in and I'm doing it anyway.'

'I'm in charge, right?' Amanda asks her father.

'Right. Don't abuse the authority.' Mr Martin

picks up his bowling ball and heads out the door.

Amanda grins evilly at her younger brother.

Matthew's day keeps getting worse and worse.

It's not even fun thinking about his upcoming birthday party any more.

Amanda goes to the phone.

For the next two hours, she is on the phone talking to her girlfriends.

Stupid girlfriends, Matthew thinks. Stupid Amanda.

It's not fair. She's going to get paid to be on the phone all night, which is something she's not allowed to do when their parents are home.

Matthew sits in his room, thinking that if he and Joshua were still friends he could have gone over to the Jackson house and not had stupid Amanda in charge. Or Joshua could come to the Martin house and they could have ganged up on Amanda by making rude noises into the extension while she was talking to her stupid friends. That it was harder to do stuff like that alone. It was more fun to gang up on her together with Joshua. She had more trouble trying to catch both of them at once.

This being mad at Joshua was no fun.

But Joshua deserved it.

Matthew only hoped that Joshua was just as miserable.

CHAPTER 7

'Open the door, nerd face. I want to talk to you.' Amanda pounds on the door.

Matthew yells, 'Stay away, baboon breath!'

Amanda is silent for a minute and then knocks on the door again.

'Go away.' Matthew is in a bad enough mood already without having his sister come in and play boss.

'Honey baby, I really have to talk to you.' Amanda pleads.

Matthew can't believe that she's calling him 'Honey baby.' She hasn't done that since they were little and he actually believed that she was going to be nice to him. He was too smart for that now.

'Honey baby.' Amanda opens the door and sticks her head in the door.

Matthew pretends that she is invisible.

In the old days, it was never safe when she said 'Honey baby' so nicely. Once she did it when she was eight and he was six and she decided to give him a 'new look.' She cut his hair all spiky, with the pinking shears, and then sprayed it bright pink. It took months for it to grow back and he was the only kid in the first grade whose mother had to dye his hair every couple of weeks. And then there was the time in second grade when she conned him out of every cent in his Fred Flintstone dino-bank so that she could get her ears pierced after their parents had told her she couldn't. They made the holes close up by not letting her put earrings in. She never repaid him and when he complained to their parents, they said it was his fault for loaning her money for something that she wasn't supposed to do.

When Matthew was little, he was very gullible when it came to his sister. Now he knew better.

'Honey baby.' Amanda comes into his room and stands by his bed, looking so sweet.

'No.' Matthew says. 'No. No. No. Absolutely not.'

'But I haven't even asked you for anything yet. How do you know that I want anything?'

'NO. NO. NO.' Matthew sticks his fingers in his ears.

Amanda tries a different method of getting to her brother. 'Listen, Pea Brain. I want you to help me.'

Now Matthew feels better. They are on familiar ground. He's used to dealing with his sister this way. He doesn't feel as defenceless with name calling as he does when she's doing her 'Honey baby' routine.

'It's going to cost you.' Matthew stares at her. 'You're going to have to give me part of the money you're going to get for babysitting me.'

Amanda says, 'That's not fair. You're getting paid too.'

'Fair? You're my sister. Who says I have to be fair to you? You never are to me.' Matthew isn't sure what they are fighting about but it doesn't matter.

'Please.' Amanda pleads, looking so sad that Matthew feels sorry for her.

'Oh, okay. I'll listen. But don't expect me to say yes.'

Amanda sits down on the edge of his bed and then jumps up because she has just sat on his Invaders of the Universe rocket ship. 'Matthew, can't you ever be neat?'

'It's my room,' he reminds her.

This time she checks before she sits down.

'Matthew, I want you to do me a favour. Could you please watch yourself for about a half an hour?'

'You want me to stand in front of a mirror and look at myself for half an hour?' Matthew grins at her. 'I don't know, Amanda, that could be very tiring.'

'You goofbrain,' Amanda says, forgetting for a second that she's trying to get him to do something for her.

'Goofbrains don't do favours for sisters.' Matthew is having fun for the first time all day.

'Honey baby, please.' Amanda really begins to beg. 'I just want to go over to Cindy's house for half an hour. It's very important.'

Cindy is Joshua's older sister. Cindy's house . . . that's Joshua's house, too.

Matthew thinks, maybe I should say yes, it's okay. And then I should wire Amanda with a bomb that will go off when she gets over there. That would solve a lot of my problems . . .

Matthew thinks about it for a minute and knows that that is too awful and disgusting a thing to do, even to Amanda and Joshua.

'Please,' Amanda begs.

'Why?' Matthew wants the details.

'Because,' Amanda tells him.

'Tell me.' Matthew knows he's got his sister exactly where he wants her.

'Oh, okay.' She relents. 'I'll tell you. But you've got to promise not to tease me or anything.'

'I promise.' Matthew is not sure if he will keep the promise; after all it is only to his sister.

'You'd better.' Amanda glares at him, forgetting for a second that she really wants something from him. 'This Friday is very special.'

'I know. It's my birthday party,' Matthew says.

'No,' she says. 'Really special. You have a birthday every year. That's not so special.'

Matthew gets ready to tell her why it's very special, but she doesn't give him the chance.

'*Really* special. There's a school dance . . . and Danny Cohen asked me to go with him.'

Danny Cohen: that's David's step-brother . . . David, who is in my class, Matthew thinks. I hear

45

that Danny's really a nice guy. Why does he want to go out with my sister? I wonder if insanity runs in his family. I'd better ask David tomorrow.

'And I have to go over to Cindy's house to try on some clothes so I have something to wear on Friday. I have nothing to wear!'

'Nothing to wear.' Matthew picks up the rocket ship and pretends to be dive bombing at her head. 'Nothing to wear! You have so many clothes that they don't fit into your wardrobe. You have to use the hall cupboard too.'

'I have nothing *new* to wear. Nothing special. I'm going to wear something of Cindy's and she's going to wear something of mine. That way it'll be like we've each got new clothes.' Amanda sighs. 'I don't know why I'm trying to explain this to you. You don't even care about clothes. You're the kid who went away to camp and never changed your underwear for an entire week.'

'That was a long time ago,' Matthew tells her.

'Yeah. Last summer.' Amanda pushes her glasses back on the bridge of her nose.

'You can go over to Cindy's house,' Matthew tells her. 'It's going to cost you, though. Half of whatever you make tonight babysitting.'

'A quarter,' Amanda bargains. 'I've decided to spend it on a new pair of shoes. Real high heels. And I won't have enough money if I have to give half of it to you.'

'Half. Take it or leave it.'

Amanda looks at her watch and realises that the

longer it takes to compromise the less time she'll have at the Jacksons'. 'Okay, okay,' she relents. 'And you promise not to tell the parents.'

'Promise.' Matthew thinks about how he can use the babysitting money to buy more stuff for the goody bags . . . that he'll use it to buy Almond Joys, Joshua's favourites. Then he remembers that he and Joshua are no longer friends.

'Thanks, Matthew. I really appreciate this.' Amanda sounds like a normal person. 'And Matthew, one more thing . . . '

Matthew grins. Another favour. It's going to cost her.

'Matthew.' Amanda continues. 'Cindy and I were talking —'

'I know. That's all you two ever do,' Matthew teases her. 'Yak. Yak. Yak.'

'Shut up and listen for a minute. Cindy and I were talking about you and Joshua and the fight. She said that Joshua is really unhappy about it, and I can tell that you are, too.'

'Am not.' Matthew shakes his head and folds his arms across his chest.

'You are, too. I can tell.' Amanda pushes her glasses up again. 'Cindy told me what happened. It really did sound like an accident. You and Joshua have been friends for too long to act like this to each other. I remember when Cindy and I had a fight in sixth grade. It was really dumb. Look, I'm older than you are. I have more experience in stuff like this. Listen to me. It was only a dumb invitation.'

47

'I'd worked on it for hours. It was the best invitation ever.'

'Matthew. I know that computers are important to you, and how good you are on them. You're better than almost anyone I know. But it's also important to have friends. You can't play ball outside with a computer, or have a real-friends type of talk with a computer. A computer can't share junk food with you.' Amanda looks at her watch. 'I've got to go. Think about what I said. Your dumb birthday party is important to you. Are you going to ruin it by not having your best friend there? That'll turn this whole thing into a big deal.'

'Why are you telling me this?'

'You're my brother,' she shrugs. 'Sometimes, weird as it seems, I even like you. Look, I've got to go. Promise that if our parents get back you'll call and warn me.'

'I promise.' Matthew nods.

'Bye.' Amanda jumps off the bed and rushes off.

'One more thing, turkey!' Matthew calls out.

'Yes?' Amanda stops.

'Keep all of the stupid babysitting money. You can buy your stupid high heels. Even though you'll probably break your stupid neck wearing them.' Matthew can hardly believe that he is saying this.

Amanda comes back, gives him a kiss on the forehead, and then rushes out.

Matthew wipes the kiss off his forehead and wonders if he's been possessed by a devil who is making him so generous.

Then he thinks about what Amanda said.

Maybe she's right.

Maybe she isn't.

Maybe he will talk to Joshua tomorrow.

Maybe he won't.

Whoever said that being a kid was easy never had a best friend, or a sister and would never be invited to Matthew's birthday party, not ever.

CHAPTER 8

'That breakfast is really gross.' Amanda looks down at her brother's plate. 'How *can* you eat granola with ketchup?'

'Easy.' Matthew grins. 'With a spoon.'

'Ha, ha.' Amanda looks up at her brother. 'You wouldn't be able to do that if Mom and Dad were here.'

'But they aren't. You know that they both had to go to work early. And Mom made me promise to eat the granola. I really hate it. I really like ketchup. I'd rather mix it with vanilla ice cream and chocolate syrup but since we can only have that stuff on special occasions, I put ketchup on it.' Matthew puts some in his mouth. 'Friday, I will actually be able to have some ice cream, syrup and cake *because*—'

'I know. I know. *Because* it's going to be your birthday.' Amanda makes herself some wholewheat toast. 'Really, Matthew. I can't understand why you're making such a big deal out of your birthday. After all, everybody has them.'

Matthew swirls the granola-ketchup mixture with his spoon. 'It's important. It's the one day a year when people really make a fuss over a kid. When everyone has to be nice to you, and you get a lot of presents that you could never buy for yourself. And in this family, it's one of the few times we can have junk food. When you're a kid, it's practically the biggest day of the year, except for Christmas, maybe. Did you buy me a present, Amanda?'

She looks at him. 'You are so greedy.'

'Yes.' He grins. 'So what did you get me?'

'I'm not telling.' She puts grape jelly on her toast.

'So you did buy me a present.' Matthew claps his hands. 'Tell me what it is.'

'Matthew. Stop it.' Amanda pulls her brother's hair. 'Stop being a pest. And hurry up, you're going to be late for school. Mom made me promise that I'd be sure to get you out of here on time.'

Matthew stares down at the breakfast that he has hardly eaten.

'Get going. And thanks for not squealing on me. I owe you one.' Amanda puts the toast into her mouth.

'Good.' Matthew tries to get her to pay up immediately. 'If you owe me one, would you please eat my breakfast for me?'

Amanda looks down at the granola-ketchup mixture and says, 'Not a chance. I'd be sick.'

Matthew picks up the bowl. 'I have an idea.'

'Just don't be late for school or you're going to be

dead meat.' Amanda shakes her finger at him. 'I've got to go to school now. Cindy and I are getting to school early. We have to talk.'

Matthew thinks about all of the talking they did yesterday, first on the phone and then in person, and thinks about how much girls gab. He was sure that Danny Cohen and whatever sucker was taking Cindy to the dance were not spending all this time talking about what they were going to wear and junk like that.

Amanda leaves.

Matthew looks down at his breakfast and knows that when his mother comes home, she's going to check the dustbin to see if he ate the granola.

He thinks of flushing it down the toilet, but knows that he can't. The last time he tried that, the five grain eggplant souffle blocked up the toilet. So no toilet stuffing allowed.

Putting the breakfast in a polythene bag, he takes it and his books and lunch outside. He grabs a shovel out of the garage and buries the breakfast bag under a bush in the front garden.

He debates burying his spelling book too, but realises that's not a good idea.

Matthew is so intent on burying the evidence that he doesn't realise that Joshua is standing behind him, watching the whole thing.

'Ashes to ashes. Dust to dust.' Matthew remembers what he saw on television once. 'The next thing I'll bury is wholewheat crust.'

'That is so lame.' Joshua starts to laugh.

Matthew looks at his friend and stands up. 'Hi,' he says quietly.

Both boys just look at each other and then both say, 'I'm sorry,' at the same time.

Then Joshua punches Matthew on his arm, not a fight punch but a friend punch.

Matthew does the same to Joshua.

The fight is over.

'We'd better get to school,' Matthew says, grabbing his books and lunch. 'We don't want detention. We have to plan for the party.'

'Okay. Race you.' Joshua starts to run.

I'll never keep up, Matthew thinks, but Joshua doesn't run as fast as he can, so the two boys run side by side.

'I brought an extra pack of cupcakes today.' Joshua holds up his lunch bag. 'You can have them unless your Mom packed you something better.'

The thought of the cupcakes makes Matthew sprint even faster. 'She packed tofu sunflower seed brownies. Even though it's going to be a sacrifice, I'll give them up for the cupcakes.'

As they near the school playground, Matthew thinks about something they'd learned in school, about how Indians used to pass the peace pipe when they wanted a war to end.

With Matthew and Joshua, it was peace cupcakes instead.

Matthew was glad the fight was over . . . with or without the cupcakes.

Planning the party was going to be fun again.

CHAPTER 9

'I'm in deep trouble, deep deep trouble,' Brian Bruno informs the guys. 'I'm not sure that I'm ever going to be allowed out of my house again, except for school and church.'

'What did you do?' Mark asks.

Brian starts to grin. 'You know my little sister, Fritzie the Pain?'

Everyone knew Fritzie. Before she learned to talk, she learned to bite. Each boy had at least one scar on his leg to remind him of Fritzie. Four years younger, Fritzie was a real pain . . . in a real way.

Brian continues. 'You know how she's always following us around, butting in?'

Everyone nods.

'Well, I decided to get even. So I trained her,' Brian tells them.

'Trained her not to bite? Trained her to give herself a rabies injection?' says Patrick Ryan, looking down at his ankle where there is still a Fritzie scar.

'No such luck,' Brian shakes his head. 'No, I trained her to do something else. Every time I said, "Who am I?" She would have to say, "King Brian, the terrific." And then I would say, "Who are you?" and she would say, "Fang Face, pig Brain, Fritzie."'

'Great,' says Mark. 'I'll have to teach that to my little sister.'

'No way.' Brian shakes his head. 'My parents heard us and they got mad, told me that I was the oldest and should know better, that I was being mean and had to be punished.'

'Oh, no. You can't come to my party,' says Matthew, who knows how Fritzie must feel being the youngest, but still sides with Brian.

'I begged them. I got down on my knees and pleaded with them to let me go,' Brian says. 'I promised them if I could go, I'd give Fritzie my goodie bag, that I'd take her to the movies two times without complaining, that I would never call her Fang Face again.'

'What happened next?' Matthew needs to know.

'I apologised to the little snaggletoothed creep in front of my parents and they said that I could go to the party, that my punishment wouldn't start until after the sleepover and then the punishment would start. So no one have a party for the next month, okay?'

Matthew thinks about how hard it is for brothers and sisters to get along; about the time he dropped water balloons on Amanda's head and she screamed, 'I will not use force on you. I will use verbal!' Sisters sure are strange.

Mrs Stanton walks into the room. 'Class, everyone sit down quietly.'

Trouble, Matthew thinks. I have a feeling that there is something I have not done.

Once everyone is seated, Mrs Stanton says, 'Who would like to hand out the paper?'

'Oh. Oh. Oh.' Jil! is practically jumping over the top of her desk, frantically waving her hand.

'Ryma. Please pass out the papers.' Mrs Stanton turns to the quietest child in the class.

Once the papers are on everyone's desk, Mrs Stanton says, 'Number from one to twenty.'

The spelling test! Matthew remembers, but he remembers too late to do anything about it.

Ten minutes later, everyone puts his or her pencil down on the desk.

Matthew's paper is a mess. It's so erased that there are holes in the paper. There are crossouts. Smudge marks. It looks like it's been in the hands of a dirty demento.

'Exchange papers with the person to the right of you,' Mrs Stanton tells them.

Matthew groans. He has to give his to Vanessa Singer. She hasn't liked him since the time he put the class gerbil in her Barbie lunchbox. It's not that he expects her to cheat for him. He just hopes that she doesn't scream out his grade. Maybe she'll be nice.

No such luck.

'Has anyone else got fifteen wrong . . . or has

Matthew won the Spelling Booby Prize again?' she yells out.

'Vanessa. That isn't very nice.' Mrs Stanton looks at her. 'How would you feel if someone did that to you?'

Vanessa sticks her nose up in the air, and shakes her curly red hair. 'There's no way that could happen to me. I would never get that many spelling words wrong. *Never*.'

Matthew wants to murder her.

He also wants to die of embarrassment.

It's not fair.

Why is spelling so important?

His computer program beeps and changes wrong spellings, so why are they bothering with these stupid spelling tests anyway?

Finally, the agony ends and the class has independent reading time.

Matthew pretends to read but actually thinks of ways to get even with Vanessa.

He can feel something start to rumble inside his body.

He debates asking for a cloakroom pass but decides against it.

Instead, he sits at his desk and expells the gas in Vanessa's direction, one of those SBDs, Silent But Deadly. Then he immediately holds his nose and calls out, 'Oh, yuck. Vanessa. How could you do that? You're so disgusting.'

Everyone in the class turns around and looks at Vanessa.

'I didn't do anything. You did, you disgusting pig.' Vanessa is blushing.

Matthew puts on his most innocent look, his most hurt look. 'Me? Why don't you just confess? I'm sure it was an accident. Don't be so ashamed.'

Everyone near them starts moaning and holding their noses.

Vanessa gets redder and redder.

Matthew is having a great time.

Vanessa looks like she's going to cry.

Matthew feels a little bit guilty until he remembers how she told everyone what a dope he was in spelling.

This will teach her.

Matthew may not be the world's best speller but he has just made everyone think that Vanessa is the world's worst smeller.

Next time Vanessa will think twice before she messes with me, Matthew thinks.

Little does he know that Vanessa is already plotting her revenge.

CHAPTER 10

Amanda Martin Cohen
Amanda Cohen
Mrs. Amanda Cohen
Mrs. Danny Cohen
Ms. Amanda Martin
Mandy Cohen
Mrs. Amanda Martin-Cohen
Mandy Martin
Mandy Martin Cohen
Amanda M. Cohen
A. Martin Cohen
Mrs. Daniel Cohen
Mr. & Mrs. Danny Cohen
Mr. & Mrs. Daniel Cohen
Mrs. and Mr. Dan Cohen

Matthew feels like he's struck gold. He's got the blackmail evidence of the century!

Going through Amanda's school notebook to get some paper, he has found the list.

Mrs Stanton said that he had to write each mis-spelled word ten times.

Ten times fifteen words. That's going to take a lot of paper.

Mrs Stanton had warned him.

He is not to do it using his computer, writing it once and having the computer repeat it fourteen more times.

He did that last time.

This time she says that if he does it again, he's going to have to handwrite each word twenty-five times.

Twenty-five times fifteen is more than Matthew cares to compute.

So he was prepared to write it out, using cursive.

However, he's left his notebook at school.

Going into the kitchen to look for paper, he has found Amanda's notebook.

It's like striking gold.

He can really blackmail her with this.

He's sure that she'd be willing to write fifteen spelling words ten times each rather than have anyone see what she's been doing.

Matthew is sure that all he is going to have to do is threaten her with giving the paper to David Cohen, who will then give it to his step-brother, Danny.

Amanda walks into the room, just as he begins to pull the page out of the notebook.

'What are you doing, you little runt?'

Matthew holds up the page.

'Wait until Danny sees this!'

Amanda rushes towards Matthew, backing him against the refrigerator.

He ducks under her arm.

Sometimes being a runt has its advantages.

However, he ducks right into his father, who is behind Amanda.

Getting his son into a headlock, Mr Martin says, 'Hi, boy. What's going on?'

'Nothing,' Matthew says. 'How about letting me go, Dad? I have some spelling homework to do.'

'Kill him!' Amanda screams. 'Break his stupid little runt neck! He's stolen something very important of mine.'

Mr Martin, who does not believe in physical violence, shakes his head.

The hold on Matthew is not strong but Matthew knows better than to try to break away.

'Drop it.' Amanda sounds ready to do serious harm.

Matthew grins at her. 'Mrs —'

'Shut up.' She pulls his hair.

'Let go,' Mr Martin says. 'Matthew. You let go of your sister's paper. Amanda. You let go of your brother's hair.' Matthew lets go of the paper.

Amanda lets go of his hair.

Mr Martin lets go of Matthew.

'Now what's going on here?' Mr Martin wants to know.

Matthew knows that if Amanda squeals, he's going to be in trouble. He also knows that if

Amanda squeals, he's going to have to tell about her leaving the house the other night while she was supposed to be babysitting.

Amanda knows that if she squeals on Matthew, he's going to squeal on her.

'It's all right, Dad. I'm not going to press charges.' Amanda has been watching People's Court.

'Are you sure?' Mr Martin asks.

'I'm sure.' Amanda sighs.

Mr Martin looks down at his son. 'Matthew. I'm not sure what you were up to but I have a feeling that you were up to no good. Watch your step, son.'

Matthew knows that he's going to need his father's help in setting up the tent for the sleepover, so he uses his most innocent look and says, 'Yes, sir.'

Mr Martin, remembering how he and his sister always used to fight when they were little, looks at his two children. He only hopes that some day they will learn to get on together, just the way he and his sister, their Aunt Nancy, now get along.

Matthew looks at Amanda.

It doesn't look like she's too happy with him.

However, he decides to press his luck.

'Can I borrow some paper from you? I need it to do my homework.' Matthew asks.

Amanda debates stepping on his head but then looks at her father who senses that she wants to step on Matthew's head and is going to make sure that doesn't happen.

'Oh, okay. What do you need?' She opens her notebook, careful that only empty pages are showing.

'Five pages,' he tells her.

'Spelling words again.' She shoves the paper at him. 'Next time, ask first.'

'Okay.' Matthew takes the paper and leaves.

Amanda looks at her father. 'He's such a child.'

Mr Martin remembers that it was only a week ago that his daughter said, 'It's not fair. I'm only a kid,' when she was asked to help clean up the house.

Amanda sits down on the kitchen stool. 'Daddy, can't you help me convince Mom that I need contact lenses?'

'No way.' Her father shakes his head.

'Plastic surgery?' she persists.

He shakes his head again.

'For my date with Danny, can I have him meet me at Cindy's house? It's going to be awful having him meet me here with that stupid party going on. Matthew is going to do something terrible to embarrass me. I know he will. Please, Daddy? Oh, please.' Amanda puts her head down on the kitchen table.

'Get up, honey.' Mr Martin runs his hand over the back of her head.

'Not until you help me with this problem.' Amanda is hard to hear because she is talking into the table.

Mr Martin thinks for a minute and then says,

'Your mother and I want Danny to come here. You can't deprive us of seeing you go out on your first date. However, I do know that there is a chance that Matthew may try to do something embarrassing.'

Mr Martin is remembering his sister's first date and how he rigged up the stereo system so that as they walked out of the door, 'Here Comes the Bride' played loudly enough for the whole neighbourhood to hear it.

'I'll talk to him, warn him, I promise,' Mr Martin tells her.

Amanda raises her head. 'Thanks, Dad.'

Getting up, she gives her father a hug.

As she leaves the room, she says, 'Tell him if he's not good, we're going to give all his presents away. That should do it.'

Mr Martin says, 'I'll take care of it.'

Amanda walks upstairs and heads directly to Matthew's room. 'Listen, you little brat, if you ever tell anyone about that page, you are dead meat.'

Matthew smiles at her.

'I'm not kidding.' She stares at him. 'If you do anything when Danny picks me up, I'm going to tell everyone how, when you're upset, you still sleep with your Babar stuffed elephant, the one you got when you were a baby.'

'I don't and you know it.' Matthew stands up.

'You know that and I know that but no one else will. They'll believe me and think you are a nerd to the Nth degree.' Amanda grins evilly.

Amanda knows she's got Matthew, that the kids will tease him even if it's not true. She also knows that she'd really never do that to him but he doesn't know that.

As Amanda leaves the room, Matthew sits down again.

What a day.

One hundred and fifty spelling words to write.

Amanda's threatening to turn him into the Class Geek.

And somewhere out there, Vanessa Singer is planning her revenge.

CHAPTER 11

//

*****ATTENTION*****ATTENTION*****ATTENTION*****ATTENTION*****ATTENTION****

\\

We, the girls of Grade Six of E.E.E., do hereby form an organisation called GET HIM, which is short for Girls Eager To Halt Immature Matthew.

We plan to do everything possible to make Matthew Martin's life as miserable as he has made ours.

SO MATTHEW MARTIN, WATCH OUT!!!!!!!!!!!!!!!!!!!!!!!!!!!!!!!!

THE GET HIM EXPLANATION:

Just so people don't think that we are being unfair gang-ing up on Matthew Martin, fink of Califon, fink of New Jersey, fink of the United States. North America. Earth. The Universe. Matthew Martin, slimeball of all eternity, we do hereby list just a few of the sneaky, disgusting, and rotten things that he has done to us!

1. Putting ketchup and mayonnaise in his mouth, puffing up his cheeks, smacking them to make the goop come out of his face onto Cathy Atwood's brand—new dress, and screaming, "I'm a zit! I'm a zit!"

2. Always making fun of Jessica Weeks's last name, saying dumb things like "Jessica Weeks makes many daze." And whenever he sees her with her parents and little sister, yelling out, "Look! It's the Month family——Four Weeks equals one month." Enough is enough!

3. Rolling up rubber cement into tiny balls, labelling them "snot balls," and putting them into Lisa Levine's pencil box.

4. Ever since preschool, kicking the bottom of the chair of the person who is unlucky enough to be seated in front of him.

5. Whenever anyone taller stands up in front of him, yelling, "I can't see through you. What do you think, that your father's a glazier?" We can't help it if practically everyone in the class is taller than Matthew. It's especially mean when he does it to Katie Delaney. She can't help it if she's the tallest person in the class.

6. Putting a "Sushi for Sale" sign in the class aquarium.

7. Teasing any boy who wants to talk to one of the girls, acting as if it were the crime of the century. Just wait until Matthew gets old enough and acts more mature (if that ever happens, especially since he is the baby of the class) and wants to ask some girl out on a date. No one in this class is ever ever going to go out with him. We've made a solemn promise as part of GET HIM. He's going to have to ask out some girl who is presently in preschool or not even born yet because we have also made a solemn promise to inform every girl in the world to WATCH OUT!

8. During the Spring Concert quietly singing the theme song from that ancient TV show <u>Mr Ed</u> while everyone else was trying to sing the correct songs.

9. Putting Bubble Yum in Zoe Alexander's very very long blonde hair, so that her mother had to spend four hours rubbing ice cubes on it, and then, when told about what a pain it was, said, "I guess that helped you cool off, you hot-head."

67

10. On last year's class trip to the Bronx Zoo, going up
to the attendants, pointing to all the girls, and saying that
they had escaped from the monkey cages.

11. Bothering all the girls at lunchtime to make them
swap their meals for the sprouty stuff he always brings.

12. Always acting like such a bigshot about computer
stuff, never helping out any girl who needs help, and acting
like Chloe Fulton doesn't exist because she's almost as good
as he is at it and could be even better if she didn't have
so many other interests. SO THERE!

13. For the Valentine Box, giving the girls envelopes
filled with night crawlers. Even though it was anonymous,
we all know who did it. Even if Mrs Stanton said we
couldn't prove it, we know it was Matthew because most of
the names were spelled wrong. So was the handwritten
message, LET ME WERM MY WAY INTO YOUR HART.

We, the eleven members of GET HIM, could go on forever listing all the stuff he's done to us, but we've decided to list just thirteen things. The unlucky number, thirteen, is only the beginning.

From now on Matthew Martin is going to have to watch out. We're going to make his life as miserable as he has made ours. He's never going to know when something is going to happen.

WE ARE SERIOUS!!!
WE ARE ANGRY!!
WE AREN'T GOING TO TAKE IT ANY MORE!!!!!!!!!!!!!!!!!!!!!!!!!!

SIGNED,
VANESSA SINGER, President

KATIE DELANEY, Vice President

JIL! HUDSON, Secretary

LIZZIE DORAN, Treasurer

MEMBERS: Cathy Atwood, Lisa Levine, Jessica Weeks, Zoe Alexander, Chloe Fulton, Ryma Browne, and Sarah Montgomery

69

✶ VANESSA SINGER ✶

Katie Delaney

Jill! Hudson

LiZZIE DORAN

Cathy Atwood   LISA LEVINE

Sarah Montgomery   Jessica Weeks

Ryma Browne

Zoe Alexander

CHAPTER 12

'You're in for it,' Joshua says, when the boys discover the GET HIM declaration on Matthew's desk. 'I'm glad that I'm not you.'

'Me too,' says Tyler White. 'But then I'm always glad that I'm not you. I'm glad I'm not you when we're playing Keepaway. I'm glad I'm not you when we're opening up our lunches. I'm glad —'

'Shut up,' Matthew says.

Tyler continues, 'And I'm really glad that I'm not you today. When all the girls gang up on someone, it's awful.'

Matthew looks at the Declaration that has been stuck to his desk with plastic imitation 'dog do' and then he looks up at Tyler again. 'Shut up.'

'Really original.' Tyler smiles at him.

'You only wish you were me when we're playing with the computer or Nintendo.' Matthew stares at him.

Tyler stares back, but he's the first one to blink and look away.

Matthew smiles for the first time since he's got

into the classroom and seen what's on his desk.

All the boys in the class are crowding around his desk.

All the girls are standing by the aquarium, talking to each other and looking his way.

Some of the girls are giggling.

Others are glaring.

Vanessa Singer looks very proud of herself.

Matthew looks round the classroom and tries to figure out what to do next.

The girls keep glaring and giggling.

Matthew is in deep trouble and he knows it.

He's not going to let anyone else know that he knows it.

Mrs Stanton walks into the room and looks round.

Everyone tries to look very innocent. They immediately head for their desks, very quietly.

Mrs Stanton looks round, trying to figure out what's going on without making too big a deal of it.

She looks at Matthew, who she figures has probably done something.

He is putting away the incriminating evidence, the plastic dog do and the declaration.

It's going right into his backpack.

There's no way that he's going to be a squealer.

That just isn't done in the sixth grade at E.E.E.

It's okay to tell on a brother or sister at home but not to tell on a classmate at school, as long as it's not a serious thing, the kind of thing that kids really should tell grownups.

This is not a serious thing. It's serious, but not SERIOUS, like drugs or abuse or something dangerous.

There's no way that he's going to act like a baby and have Mrs Stanton take care of it by talking to the girls. That would only make things worse, and Matthew Martin has a feeling that things are going to be bad enough as it is.

Vanessa Singer keeps sneaking looks at him and snickering.

'Would you like to share the joke with us, Vanessa dear?' Mrs Stanton says stuff like that a lot when she wants kids to stop fooling around.

It works.

Vanessa takes her notebook out of her desk and looks at the next spelling list.

So does everyone else.

There is a lot of giggling going around.

Not just the girls, but the boys, too.

All of the boys except Matthew, who is beginning to wonder if he's finally going to be paid back for all the things he has done to other people.

Matthew goes into his desk to take out his spelling list.

Someone has put cling film wrap over all the stuff in his desk and covered the wrap with lime jelly. It keeps wiggling back and forth.

It looks so gross.

Matthew wishes he had thought of doing it . . . to someone else, probably to Vanessa Singer. But he would have added little pieces of his mother's tofu, which would have made it look really gross.

But he didn't think of it. Someone else had, and now it was in Matthew's desk, looking like the Slime That Ate Califon.

Green jelly was the only flavour he hated. Someone who knew his habits was out to get him.

Looking round the room, he realised that there were eleven someones who were out to get him.

This wasn't fair to do to someone with a birthday coming up, someone who was going to be very busy getting ready for his party, someone who didn't want to waste his time thinking about what a bunch of dumb girls were going to do to him.

Maybe this will be it, Matthew thinks. Maybe the dumb girls have had their dumb fun and they'll leave me alone.

Three minutes later, Matthew feels someone kicking the bottom of his chair.

He turns around to check it out.

It's Lizzie Doran . . . and she's smiling.

CHAPTER 13

'Matthew. Something seems to be bothering you lately.' Mr Martin looks up from the book he is reading.

'It's nothing.' Matthew shakes his head and continues to doodle all over his maths homework.

'Are you sure?' Mr Martin stares at his son. 'You know you can tell me anything. And now is a good time with your mother and your sister out shopping for an outfit for the dance.'

Matthew draws a skull and crossbones on the paper and labels it POIZON: FOR SIXTH GRADE GIRLS. 'No. No trouble at all.'

He looks down at the paper and thinks about how rotten everything has been lately; how all the girls are making his life absolutely miserable, how most of the other boys don't want to start an anti-girl club, how even Joshua won't do it, and how Joshua had said, 'The girls aren't against all of us, just you. And Matthew, you've got to admit it, they do have their reasons to be mad at you.'

Matthew thinks about all the stuff he's done to

the girls, but he also thinks about how he's done stuff to everyone. It's not that he's especially against the girls, it's just that school gets so boring sometimes that he's got to do something to liven it up. He thinks about how all of the girls have been against him for three days now, kicking his seat, putting signs on his back saying things like 'SO DUMB HE SPELLS IT DUM' and 'G.E.T. H.I.M. wants you to KICK HIM.' He thinks about how someone's putting messages into the computer saying things like 'MATTHEW MARTIN IS NOT USER FRIENDLY' and 'WATCH OUT . . . WE'RE GOING TO PUT A MAGNET NEXT TO ALL YOUR DISCS AND WIPE THEM OUT', and how Jil! Hudson has been doing really terrible things like telling everyone that they are engaged and that he is secretly going steady with her, then making these disgusting barfing noises and all of the girls giggle.

'Son. Are you sure you're all right? You haven't mentioned your party once today. Your mother and I are getting a little concerned.' Mr Martin puts down his book.

Shaking his head, Matthew says, 'It's all right, Pop. Honest.'

All Right, Matthew thinks, Ha! All Right. There are eleven people picking on me. It's not fair. So, it's true. Sometimes I do things to other people, but I don't mean to be really mean. I don't gang up on anyone, and I have eleven people against me all at once. But what's the use of telling anyone?

'Matthew.' Mr Martin stands up. 'I've been

thinking. As one of your birthday presents, your mother and I were going to give you a bubble-making set, with instructions for making huge bubbles, for doing lots of tricks. Why don't you and I take that present out now and try some stuff out so that you can use it at your birthday party?'

Matthew smiles. Finally.

Mr Martin says, 'I'll go get the bubbles. Don't follow me. I don't want you to know where the secret hiding place is.'

As his father leaves, Matthew smiles again.

He knows where the secret hiding place is, where all the secret hiding places are.

After all, when a person has spent his entire life living in one house, it's easy to figure out stuff like that unless, of course, you are a prince or princess and live in a huge castle. There are probably millions of places in a castle to hide things but most people, Matthew is sure, live in places where anyone can figure out the hiding places after almost eleven years of life. And Matthew has figured them out.

Sometimes stuff is hidden in the old trunk in the attic. Sometimes, if it's small enough, it's in his mother's drawer where she keeps her nightgowns. Sometimes it's in the garage, hidden behind the rakes and stuff, where the parents are sure no kid is going to look. Once, at Christmas, they even hid stuff in boxes in the freezer. Since his mother had labelled it LIVER, Matthew never found it.

Matthew is sure that the bubble stuff is on the top

shelf of his father's wardrobe, behind the scarves.

He sneaks into his parents' bedroom and spies on his father who is taking the present out of the clothes hamper in the bathroom.

Wrong, Matthew thinks, but at least I know another hiding place.

Matthew quietly rushes back into the living room, jumping on the couch and landing in a horizontal position. He stares up at the ceiling as if he's been lying there for hours.

Carrying the package into the living room, Mr Martin says, 'We'd better do this outside. Your mother's going to have a cow if we get soap all over the furniture.'

As they head outside, Matthew thinks about some of the weird stuff his parents say.

His father is always saying, 'Your mother's going to have a cow if . . . ' When Matthew was little he used to wonder where they were going to put the cow if his mother actually had it. He always hoped that it would go into Amanda's room, where it would sleep in her bed and keep her awake all night mooing. But his mother never did have a cow, even if she did get pretty angry sometimes.

In the front yard, Matthew and his father pour the bubble mixture into a large aluminium baking pan and then make large wands, using coat hangers with string wrapped around them.

The bubbles are huge.

Matthew only wishes he could make them big enough to put a dumb sixth grade girl inside each one and float them all up to Mars, or at least over Budd Lake so that some bird could peck the bubbles and the girls would plop into the water.

Just as Matthew starts to say something, one of Mr Martin's bubbles travels across the lawn and lands on Matthew, breaking right on his face.

'*Yug.*' The taste of the bubbles is not wonderful nor is the sticky feeling all over his face.

Mr Martin starts to laugh and moves closer, blowing more bubbles at Matthew, using a smaller wand.

This is war.

Matthew runs over to the box, takes out another small wand and starts blowing bubbles into his father's face.

His father is winning until Matthew gets a lot of liquid into the wand and blows so hard that there's no bubble, just liquid glob all over his father's face.

This is more than war. It's annihilation.

Mr Martin grabs his son's foot, pulls him to the ground and sits on him.

Then he takes the wand and keeps blowing bubbles all over Matthew's face.

Matthew can't stop laughing.

He also can't manage to get the wand away from his father.

'Boys.' Mrs Martin arrives on the scene.

Amanda is right behind her. 'You two are so gross.'

Mr Martin blows bubbles towards her. 'I am not gross. I am your father.'

'Mother. Make them stop. Everyone can see them. What if one of my friends comes by?' Amanda sighs. 'It's bad enough that my brother is so immature . . .'

'Young lady. You'd better stop before you say anything else.' Mr Martin continues to blow bubbles at her and then starts blowing them at his wife. He is still sitting on his son.

'Stop. You're getting me all sticky.' Mrs Martin is laughing.

'You ain't seen nothing yet.' Mr Martin gets off his son and starts moving towards his wife. He's picked up the very large wand.

Mrs Martin moves towards the tap where the garden hose is attached.

'I'm getting out of here.' Amanda clutches the packages containing her new clothes and runs into the house. 'You are all nuts!'

'Nuts?' We're your parents, not nuts,' Mr Martin tells his daughter and then turns back to Mrs Martin. 'Come here, my little cashew.'

Matthew watches as his mother holds up the hose and says, 'Michael Martin. I'm warning you. I've known you since second grade and there are days I don't think you've changed all that much since then. If you blow bubbles at me once more, you're going to be sorry. Very sorry.'

'I dare you.' Mr Martin grins, moves closer and blows bubbles at her.

She aims the hose at her husband and turns the water on.

Soaked, he drops the bubbles and runs over to try to capture the hose.

Amanda sticks her head out the window. 'Would you all stop? Please, you are so embarrassing.'

Matthew watches as his mother continues to spray his father until his father captures the hose and sprays his mother.

Amanda, in the background, is pleading for her parents to stop.

Soaked, Mr and Mrs Martin look at each other and laugh.

Then they hug each other, kiss and then whisper something to each other.

Matthew is standing there, watching the whole thing.

After they whisper, his father hands the hose to Mrs Martin and starts walking over to Matthew.

Both parents are grinning.

Matthew can tell he's going to get it.

As he tries to run, his father catches up and pulls him down to the ground again.

His mother rushes over with the hose, sprays Matthew and then sprays Mr Martin again.

The three of them are laughing.

Mrs Martin looks down at the two very wet men in her family and says, 'Maybe you guys should go take a nap right now and say a little prayer, like, "Now I spray me down to sleep."'

Mr Martin groans at the pun.

Matthew says, 'I think we should buy a water bed.'

Mr Martin stands and reaches his hand down to help his son get up.

Mrs Martin turns off the hose.

Matthew gets up.

His mother hugs him.

He hugs her back.

He's beginning to feel like the old Matthew, before the girls ganged up on him.

Amanda sticks her head out of the window again. 'Would you all come into the house? Please.'

'Join us.' Mr Martin uses a funny teasing voice.

Looking at her family as if she thinks they should all check into a roach motel, Amanda shakes her head and vanishes into the house.

Mrs Martin says, 'Inside, before we catch pneumonia.'

As they squish their way back inside, Matthew thinks about how this has been the best day in a very long time, how those dumb girls have driven him nuts long enough, how the old Matthew is back again.

Those dumb girls better watch out.

Instead of G.E.T. H.I.M., it's going to be G.E.T. T.H.E.M.:

GIRLS EASY TO TORMENT HOPES EVIL MATTHEW.

CHAPTER 14
WAYS TO GET EVEN
By Matthew Martin

1.

Put Silly Putty in Cathy Atwood's baloney sandwich.

2.

Next time Lizzie Doran kicks the back of my chair, grab her foot and not let go of it. Also, pretend to be looking under my chair for something and tie her laces together so that when she stands up, she won't be able to walk.

3.

Take the large science magnet and see if it can attach to all the girls who wear braces.

4.

Put a whoopie cushion on Vanessa Singer's chair.

5.

Make puking noises in Lisa Levine's ear. It always makes her sick.

6.

Since Sarah Montgomery has a horse, act like she smells like one. Say things like "Howdy, NEIGHbour." Sniff when I am near her, saying, "Hay. What did you step in?"

7.

Next time Jill Hudson says that we are going to get married, tell her that the only one dum enough to marry her would be King Kong because he's a big ape just like she is.

8.

Tell Jimmy Sutherland, the fifth-grader that Chloe has a crush on, that she has the creeping crud.

9.

Stand behind Zoe Alexander and ask, "What goes one hundred miles an hour backwards?" and then blow my snot back up my nose. That always gets her.

10.

Pretend to take my eyeball out of my face and into my mouth and wash it. That grosses out all the girls.

11.

Put a sign on Vanessa Singer's desk. YOU CAN PICK YOUR FRIENDS . . . YOU CAN PICK YOUR NOSE . . . BUT VANESSA SINGER PICKS HER FRIEND'S NOSE.

When Katie Delaney is in front of the class giving
a book report, make faces at her, like trying to touch
my nose with my tongue, pulling my lower eyelids as
low as they can go, wiggling my ears. Katie busts a
gut when stuff like that happens. Do all of that
without getting caught by Mrs Stanton.

Collect belly-button lint and toe crud from all of the
boys and put it in Vanessa Singer's desk.

Matthew grins as he finishes printing up the list.

It may not be perfect. There may be more tortures
to think of doing but it's a start.

And there are thirteen on the list. Just like there
were on the dumb girls' list.

Matthew is sure that the girls are going to regret
the day that he started this war.

Leaving the computer on because he plans to get
back to it once he's got himself a little snack,
Matthew puts the printout next to the computer,
and heads for the kitchen.

Amanda and his mother are already there, doing
something at the table.

Going over to see what's going on, Matthew
looks at his mother putting artificial nails on top of
Amanda's bitten-down fingernails.

The make believe nails are bright red and
Amanda keeps grinning.

'These look so wonderful,' she gushes. 'I'm going

to look so grownup for the dance.'

She looks up at Matthew and says, 'What are you staring at, nerdface?'

Matthew does not like being called nerdface, especially when he has done nothing to deserve it.

He pretends to study Amanda's face. 'How grownup can you look when you have that giant ugly gross pimple on your chin? It looks like a volcano.'

Quickly covering her chin with her hand, Amanda's whole mood changes. 'Oh, no. What am I going to do? There are only two more days until the dance. I can't go. Mom, you have to call Danny and tell him that I have appendicitis.'

'It's only a disgusting looking pimple.' Matthew smiles at her. 'Maybe he gets turned on by pus.'

'Matthew Martin. I want you to stop teasing your sister immediately.' Mrs Martin shakes her fist at him and then turns to her daughter. 'Amanda. There is no pimple on your face. You have to stop letting your brother torment you like this.'

Amanda rushes out of the kitchen to look in a mirror.

Matthew goes over to the refrigerator, opens the door and asks, 'Anything good to eat?'

Mrs Martin says, 'Matthew. This fighting has got to stop. I'm sick and tired of the way that you tease your sister all the time.'

'Nerdface. She called me nerdface,' Matthew reminds her. 'I didn't even do anything and she called me nerdface. Do you think that was right?'

Mrs Martin sighs and sits down at the table.

Amanda rushes back into the room. 'You little nerdface. There was nothing on my face.'

'Yes, there is.' Matthew grins at her. 'There *is* something on your face. Lopsided glasses.'

'Matthew.' Mrs Martin stands up again. 'Enough — and stop calling your brother nerdface, Amanda.'

Amanda smiles.

That is not the response that Matthew expects.

She also holds up the computer printout that Matthew has left in the study.

That is definitely not something that Matthew expected either.

'Mom. I just found something you really should look at.' Amanda is trying hard to look concerned, not incredibly happy at getting back at her brother. 'This could get dear little Matthew into big trouble at school. I would never show it to you if I weren't so worried.'

Ha, Matthew thinks. Worried is not the right word.

Amanda continues, faking a very grownup voice. 'As I said, I'm only showing this to you because I don't want Matthew to do these things at school and maybe turn into a juvenile delinquent and maybe someday turn to a life of crime. It's for his own good and I only hope that he doesn't use this opportunity to make up stories about things that he wants to make you believe that I've done.'

Mrs Martin stares at her children, not positive

about the best way to handle the situation.

She wants to respect her children's privacy.

She also wants to protect them from harm.

She remembers all the times her own mother said, 'Just wait until you have children of your own.'

Amanda waves the list in front of her. 'I'm serious. This could cause a lot of trouble and torture.'

Mrs Martin sighs again. 'Amanda. Give me the paper and then go to your room. I will finish helping you with your nails later.'

Amanda smirks as she leaves the room.

Matthew watches as his mother reads the list.

Mrs Martin turns away from him so that he can't see her face.

Matthew wonders if he can convince his mother that he is just doing homework that Mrs Stanton assigned.

It's doubtful.

Mrs Martin turns back and looks at her son.

Matthew can tell by her face that even though she's trying very hard not to smile, she's not going to accept any kidding around about this, that he's going to have to explain what's really going on.

Matthew sits down to, as his father says, face the music.

He only hopes that when everything is over, his parents won't cancel the sleepover, and that the only music that he will have to face is the guys singing, 'Happy Birthday To You.'

CHAPTER 15

WHY I WILL NOT TRY TO GET EVEN BY MATTHEW MARTIN

I will not get even for many reasons.
The first one is that my parents say that if I do
I can't have my birthday party. That is really the
biggest reason that I won't try to get even.

I will also not try to get even because my parents
will make me write another composition just like this
one. I personally don't think it's a good idea to make
a kid like me write something that's not for school, just
for his parents. It's especially not grate (great) when the
kid is not a good speller and they have said that everything
should be spelled correctly. I personally believe that
there should be a seperation (separation) between home and
school.

My mother told me why I should not get even so I will
use some of her reasons so that this paper is long enough.
She said that even though some of the things seemed harm-
less, someone could get hurt with some of them, if not
fisically (phisically, physically), their feelings could
get hurt. She also said that swallowing Silly Putty could
be danjerus (dangerous), that braces are expensive to repair,
and that I seem to have an abnormel (abnormil, abnormal)
interest in snot.

I could tell that she wasn't _so_ mad, because there were times when she almost laughed out loud. But then she said how I should try to work things out more directly, maybe apologize for some of the things that had made the girls mad in the first place, and not ever do them again.

I tried to explain why that wasn't going to work (my mother doesn't realize what a crudball Vanessa Singer really is and how stubborn she can be). But I did agree to write this paper about how I won't do any of the things that I said I would do on my list.

So now that I have written this, I can have my party, right?

Signed,

Matthew Martin

'Matthew, I'm willing to accept this essay as proof of your intention to not wage war with the Girls of G.E.T. H.I.M.' Mr Martin keeps smiling, even though he is trying to look very strict. 'You will, as I understand it, give up all thoughts of G.E.T. T.H.E.M. Correct?'

'Yeah.' Matthew looks at the floor.

'Yeah?' Mr Martin lifts his son's chin. 'Yeah? Is that the way to talk while you are trying to convince your old man of the sincerity of your words? Look at me and tell me that you mean what you say.'

'Yes, sir,' Matthew sighs and looks his father in the eyes.

His father is smiling and remembering some of the things that he, himself, did when he was a kid. He is also remembering how his parents made him promise to do things that he really didn't want to do and only hopes that Matthew will really do what he has said he would do. Disciplining his children is not one of Mr Martin's favourite things about being a father.

Mr Martin ruffles his son's hair. 'Okay, your mother and I spoke to Mrs Stanton this afternoon and she has promised to talk to the girls.'

'Aw, Pop. You know I didn't want you to do that. Now everyone is going to think I'm a nerd, a complete and total nerd. Now the girls will really torture me and you've made me promise to do nothing. I'm a dead duck.'

'It'll be all right,' Mr Martin says, hoping that it will be, but not sure.

Fat chance, Matthew thinks. Mrs Stanton will tell the dumb girls that they will get detention if they do something at school but she can't control what they do off school grounds.

Matthew is sure that he is in deep, deep, deep, deep trouble. And there is nothing he can do about it since he's promised not to fight with the girls and to do nothing to Amanda for squealing on him.

Life sure isn't fair, Matthew thinks.

He's just glad that Amanda is out shopping with their mother so that she can't gloat about his problems.

He hopes that Danny Cohen regains his sanity and un-asks her to the dance and that Amanda turns into a social reject.

He tries to figure out what he can do to get back at all the girls who are making his life miserable, but it's no use. His parents have warned him, if he breaks his promises, he will have *no* more birthday parties, not ever, no allowance and two pounds of alfalfa sprouts and tofu a day. (The threat of alfalfa sprouts and tofu came from his father. His mother said, 'Your father is just kidding about that. We don't use food as a reward or punishment.') Matthew heard his father mumble that sprouts weren't just punishment, they were torture.

Torture, Matthew knows, is what the girls are going to do to him when they realise that he can't fight back.

'Matthew. Where are you? Are you daydreaming?' his father asks.

Matthew looks up. 'It's more of a nightmare.'

'How about putting the tent up? That way if there are any problems with it, we'll know about them now, instead of tomorrow, when everyone is here for the party. And it'll get your mind off your troubles.'

'Great idea,' Matthew says. 'Also, I should probably fill the goody bags tonight and sample the sweets to make sure that we aren't giving away any stale old sweets. We wouldn't want anyone to get sick and sue us for a million-billion dollars.'

Putting his hand on his son's shoulder, Mr Martin says, 'I think it's my responsibility as your father to help you test those sweets — especially the M&Ms and the liquorice, which are my personal all-time favourites.'

'It's a deal.' Matthew smiles, glad that his father is not as nutty about health food as his mother.

'Race you to the garage.' His father starts running. 'People over thirty get a head start.'

Matthew and his father race to the garage to get the tent and to pig out on sweets. It's Matthew's last day as a ten-year-old and he intends to live it up.

CHAPTER 16

'Mom. Do you promise that you aren't going to have one of those goofy people from work come over here and embarrass me? All of the guys are going to think it's so corny to have people in costumes singing and dancing and acting like goof balls.' Matthew moves his finger around the mixing bowl and picks up left over icing.

'I promise.' Mrs Martin looks up from the cake that she's decorating. 'It costs too much, even with my discount and anyway, everyone is booked this weekend. Also, I promised your sister not to do it since she is afraid that she too will die of embarrassment. I wonder when I turned into such an embarrassment for my children. Back in the old days, you used to think that I was always right, always wonderful. Look, I promise. I'm not sending anything . . . scouts' honour —'

'You're not a girl scout,' Matthew reminds her.

'Okay: mother's honour . . . wife's honour . . .

working woman's honour.'

'Mom!' Amanda calls out from her room.

'I'll be right there, honey.' Mrs Martin puts down the cake decorating tube.

'Mom.' Matthew looks at her. 'This isn't fair. You keep going into Amanda's room to help her instead of getting ready for *my* party, which is definitely much more important. The guys are going to be here any minute, *any minute* — and my cake only says Happy B. It's not fair. Amanda has been getting dressed for her stupid date for the last five hours. She keeps changing her clothes. She keeps trying on new make-up. She keeps practising trying to walk without her glasses. She keeps tripping over things and looking squinty. She's really a mess. And you keep going in to help her.'

'You only have a first date once.' Mrs Martin smiles. 'Matthew, some day you will go out on your first date and you'll care about how you look, too.'

Matthew picks up the cake decorating tube, holds it over his face and squeezes some icing into his mouth. Some of it spills on to his cheek. He wipes it off, streaking it across his face.

'On second thoughts, maybe you won't ever care.' Mrs Martin kisses him on the forehead.

'No licking it off my face.' Matthew grins.

Mrs Martin sighs. 'Matthew.'

'Mom!' Amanda yells. 'It's an emergency. I can't decide which earrings to wear.'

'Coming, honey.' Mrs Martin heads upstairs.

'Coming, honey.' Matthew softly mimics his

mother. 'Coming, honey. Of course, your stupid first date is very important, more important than my only son's birthday because . . . because you are such a dweeble that no one is ever going to ask you out again.'

Matthew looks down at the cake, then up at the clock — and thinks that the guys could arrive any time now. No one waits until the exact second the invitation says to show up. What if the guys show up and look at the cake and see only HAPPY B? They'll know that everyone in the family thinks that dumb Amanda is more important than he is.

Matthew points the decorating tube at the cake and thinks, here goes. I can do this myself.

On the cake appear the words, HAPPY BERTHDAY.

Matthew is very proud of himself for taking care of things himself.

He looks at the cake.

Something does not look right.

Matthew looks at it for a few minutes, but he isn't sure.

Amanda rushes into the kitchen, goes to the refrigerator and pulls out a can of diet soda. 'I'm never going to be ready on time.'

'You've been getting ready for weeks. I don't understand what your problem is. Anyway, I've got problems of my own.' Matthew points to the cake.

Amanda looks at it. 'Let me guess. You wrote out HAPPY BERTHDAY yourself.'

'Mom did half of it, and then she had to go and

help you.' Matthew makes a face.

Amanda debates leaving the cake the way that it is, but then thinks about how rotten Matthew is going to feel if everyone sees how 'Birthday' is mis-spelled. 'It's I, not E. Look is there any more icing left, besides what is on your face?'

Matthew hands her the mixing bowl.

Amanda looks at the clock on the wall, thinks about how she should be getting her nails on and looks back at Matthew.

It is not going to be much fun for him if all his friends tease him on his birthday.

Taking a knife out of the drawer, Amanda scrapes the E off the cake, fills in the hole with brown carob icing, and inserts the I.

'All better now.' Amanda grins at her brother. 'Happy Birthday, Creepling. Now I've got to go.'

She rushes out of the kitchen and back to her bedroom, where her mother is putting clothes back on hangers and placing them back in the wardrobe.

Matthew looks at his cake and smiles.

Amanda did a pretty good job.

Nobody is going to be reminded what a lousy speller he is.

Amanda was actually nice for a change.

There is a good chance that this party is going to be great, especially if everyone brings terrific presents, Matthew thinks.

The doorbell rings.

It's Joshua, carrying a sleeping bag and a present.

The present looks very flat, not like a toy or game or computer disk or anything good at all.

Joshua hands the present to him. 'It's a dumb shirt. My mother made me bring it. I wanted to get you a Destroyers of the Earth zap gun, but my mother said your mother wouldn't allow it in the house.'

'I wish you had brought it. I could have used it on the girls of G.E.T. H.I.M.' Matthew holds up the present and pretends that it is a zap gun.

In walks Mr Martin, carrying a large bag. 'Hi, guys. Ice cream delivery.'

'What flavour did you get? Did you get my favourite one — Bubble Gum Ripple?' Joshua asks.

Shaking his head, Mr Martin says, 'No. That was the last flavour of the month. I got double fudge with butterscotch, blueberry cheesecake . . .'

'Yuk,' say both of the boys at the same time.

'More of it for me.' Mr Martin rubs his stomach. 'It's not often that we get real ice cream into this house. So when we do I try to make the most of it. We also have Peanut Brickle, Pistachio, Chocolate Mint and Banana Royale.'

'That's enough for an army.' Joshua licks his lips.

Mrs Martin comes back into the kitchen and looks at all the ice cream that Mr Martin is showing the boys.

'All that sugar.' She sighs. 'We're going to have a group of boys spending the night with us who are all sugared up. I thought that you were going to get one flavour, maybe two.'

99

Mr Martin tries to look sorry for what he has done but it's obvious that he's not. 'They didn't have Granola Grape or Sprout Sundae as this month's flavour of the month.'

Mrs Martin shakes her head. 'I married you for better or for worse. Your food preferences are definitely not among your better qualities.'

As Mr Martin puts the ice cream into the refrigerator, the doorbell rings.

Billy Kellerman and Pablo Martinez arrive.

Mrs Martin goes outside to talk to Mrs Kellerman.

Earlier in the week, Mrs Martin had Matthew give all the boys a paper to take home. A parent was to fill out the form, saying whether the boy was allergic to anything, who to call in case of emergency, and if a boy got homesick was he to go home or stay anyway.

Mrs Martin believes in organisation.

Billy Kellerman never takes papers home.

Tyler White and Mark Ellison show up on their bikes, doing wheelies.

Brian Bruno, Patrick Ryan and David Cohen march up to the front door, with their sleeping bags on their heads, singing 'I Love A Parade'.

'Let the wild rumpus begin!' yells Joshua, using a saying from one of his favourite books from when he was a little kid, *Where the Wild Things Are*.

Everyone goes into the den.

Matthew opens the presents.

There are more baseball cards for his collection

and a new Nintendo cartridge, a couple of tapes, a magic set, a squirting calculator, the shirt that Joshua's mother picked out, a Transformer that turns into a working camera (a present sent by Matthew's grandmother in Florida), The Oozone Layer, a game that gets slime all over everyone, and more clothes, picked out by more mothers.

'Awesome!' 'Rad,' and 'Excellent,' are some of the responses as Matthew opens the package from Mark Ellison and Patrick Ryan.

In the package are suction cup bullet holes, to be put on someone's skin. Also included are capsules of make-believe blood, to be broken over the skin where the bullet holes are placed.

Matthew looks over at his mother as he unwraps some more of the items in the box.

She definitely looks underwhelmed by the presents.

Matthew only hopes that she will let him keep these gifts.

There are also some make-believe tattoos and one of those baseballs that look like a monster's eyes.

'Wow. Thanks.' Matthew puts the eye ball in front of his own eyeball.

His mother is shaking her head.

His father is laughing.

'I can use this all for my next book report.' Matthew thinks fast. 'Mrs Stanton said we should do a mystery. This stuff will come in handy for the oral report.'

'I'm sure.' Mrs Martin sounds a little sarcastic.

'Really.' Matthew puts on his most angelic look and decides to change the subject and not to pull out the last item, a skull and crossbones bike sticker. 'What's in that big box over there?'

Mr and Mrs Martin hand Matthew a large package.

Matthew rips off the wrapping paper as his mother yells, 'Save the bow. We can use it again.'

Matthew forgets and demolishes the bow, opening the package to discover a remote control car.

'Luck-y,' say several of the guys at the same time.

'Let me see that.' Tyler holds out his hands.

'Me first.' Matthew takes the car out of the box and he and his father set it up.

'This is from your sister.' Mrs Martin shows Matthew a certificate that says that Matthew now has a subscription to *Radio Control Car Action*.

'Luck-y.'

'I get first dibs on borrowing it after you're done,' Joshua says.

Mr and Mrs Martin go out of the room and some of the guys start playing with the car.

Two tournaments begin. Nintendo and Computer.

Four people play.

The rest cheer or boo.

Soon everyone goes over to the bowl of gummy worms and puts a gummy worm above his lips, pretending to be the principal, Mr Curtis, who has just started to grow a moustache.

The doorbell rings.

'I thought everyone was here already,' Matthew says, eating the tail of the gummy worm — or maybe it's the head. He's not sure.

'I think it's my brother, my step brother,' David says.

'The date,' Joshua says. 'Let's do something to get them all embarrassed.'

'My brother said he would kill me if we did anything.' David shakes his head. 'Let's not, and say we did. That way I'll still be alive to have my own birthday party in two months.'

Matthew is glad that David has said not to do anything, that he isn't the one who had to do it.

He's thinking about how, even though Amanda is a real pain sometimes, she did help him with the birthday cake and she really doesn't deserve to have her first date messed up, even though it would, in some ways, be a lot of fun to do something to her.

'You guys promise to stay in here, and I'll ask my Mom if we can have the cake and ice cream now.'

'A bribe. I'll take it,' Brian Bruno says.

Mark Ellison, who has ten gummy worms coming out of his mouth, is walking around shaking his head at everyone so that the worms look like they are alive.

Matthew goes out of the room and sees Amanda standing in the hallway. She's trying to keep her balance on her new high heels, biting her press-on nails and attempting to see without her glasses.

She's a wreck.

Matthew tries to make Amanda feel better. 'For a

goofy girl, you don't look half bad.'

Amanda smiles, a little. 'Thank you . . . I think.'

They walk into the living room.

Mr and Mrs Martin are standing there, talking to Danny, who looks a little nervous, too.

Mr Martin takes out a camera and says, 'I hope that you two don't mind, but I'd love to take a picture.'

'Oh Daddy, that's so embarrassing.' Amanda looks like she's going to die.

Danny says, 'If you're going to take a picture of anything, sir, I think you might want to take a picture of what's happening on your pavement.'

'What's happening?' Mr and Mrs Martin go immediately to the front door.

So does Amanda, who says, 'This is so gross.' She starts to giggle.

Matthew goes up to the door and looks out.

It's the girls of G.E.T. H.I.M. and they are marching back and forth, carrying picket signs and wearing t-shirts that they have decorated themselves.

The t-shirts say:

The girls of G.E.T. H.I.M. Strike Again!

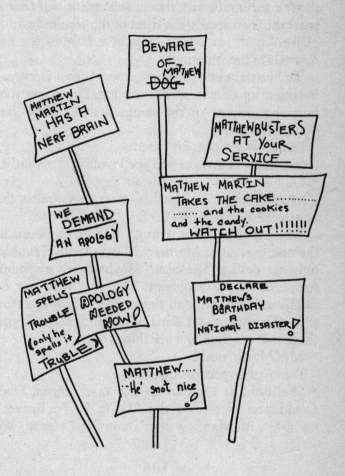

CHAPTER 17

'Oh, gross. This is so gross,' Amanda is laughing.

'They asked me to bring in a message.' Danny is laughing too, although he's also feeling a little embarrassed that there are so many people around to watch him pick up his date. 'They said that they're willing to negotiate a settlement. All that it will take is an apology in front of the whole class.'

'Apologise for what?' Matthew fails to see the humour in the situation.

'For just about everything, apparently.' Danny is having a lot of trouble not smiling. David has told him about some of the things that Matthew has done in class.

Matthew looks at his parents.

'Matthew. How do you spell trouble?' his father asks.

Closing his eyes, Matthew tries to visualise the word. 'T - R - U - B - B - L - E.'

'Well, that poster is wrong.' Mr Martin points to the one that says, Matthew Martin spells Trouble, only he spells it TRUBLE. 'Maybe that's a symbol for some of the problems. The girls may not be totally correct about all things, but they may be on the right track about some of the things. Don't you think that it's time to work things out?'

Mrs Martin nods.

Danny whispers to Amanda.

She looks at her parents and says, 'Mom. Dad. Could you please do the "Leave It To Beaver" number with Matthew after Danny and I leave? We have to go over to the Jackson's house and get our ride to the dance there.'

'Okay, Wally. We'll talk to the Beav after you go.' Mr Martin is laughing and pretending to be Mr Cleaver.

'Leave It To Beaver' is the old television show that the Martins always watch together, and at the end Mr Martin always says, 'Why can't our family be more like that? Why can't all families be more like that?'

Mrs Martin gets into the act too. 'Now, I want you to make sure that you children are careful, get home on time, and Just Say No to all the things that you know that you are to say No to. And if you see Eddie Haskell be sure to give him my regards.'

Mrs Martin always hisses when Eddie Haskell comes on the show.

Amanda looks at Danny. 'I can't help it. My family is weird. I warned you.'

'That's all right. Ever since my mother's remarriage, my family tries to be the Brady Bunch.' Danny reaches out and holds Amanda's hand. 'It could be worse. They could try to be The Munsters.'

As Amanda and Danny go out the door, the girls all start yelling things like, 'MATTHEW MARTIN, COME OUT RIGHT NOW! WE DEMAND AN APOLOGY. APOLOGISE. APOLOGISE. APOLOGISE.'

Amanda turns around and looks at Matthew.

'Thank you so much for causing all this commotion when all I want to do is have a happy memory of this.'

'It's not my fault.' Matthew goes to the door.

'It's always your fault.' Amanda trips on her high heels.

Danny catches her.

The girls catch sight of Matthew at the door. 'APOLOGISE. APOLOGISE. APOLOGISE. APOLOGISE.'

'What are you going to do?' Joshua walks into the living room.

The rest of the boys follow.

Tyler White waves to Zoe Alexander, who is his girl friend.

Cupping his hands, he calls out, 'I thought you were going over to Vanessa's to have a pyjama party!'

She calls back, 'We are, but first this.'

Vanessa Singer looks very proud of herself.

Matthew wishes that a tornado would come and take all of the girls to Kansas.

The tornado doesn't materialise.

'I think you should talk to them before the neighbours begin to complain about the noise,' Mr Martin says.

'Let them complain.' Matthew shakes his head. 'Then they'll call the cops and have the girls arrested.'

'I think that there is a better solution.' Mrs

Martin puts her hand on her son's shoulder.

'Call the F.B.I. in?' Matthew feels that would be the better solution.

'Matthew.' Mrs Martin says.

'I think you should apologise and let the girls have ice cream and cake with us,' Joshua suggests.

'No way.' Matthew shakes his head.

Pablo Martinez says, 'Come on, Matthew. The girls aren't so bad. You know that you like some of them, that you used to be friends with them.'

Matthew thinks about how hard it is to always be the youngest one in his class, how he always feels like he's playing Catch-up, how it seems like everyone is always a little ahead of him. Can he help it that he's always the youngest — in his family — and in his class?

He wishes that some new younger kid would move into town and be put in the sixth grade class.

He wishes that his parents would have another kid: a younger one, obviously.

He wonders if it's too late to ask for one, instead of the remote control car.

He wonders if he can have both, the baby brother and the remote control car.

'Matthew, you've got to do something.' Billy Kellerman points to the girls, who are now sitting on the lawn with their arms linked, singing an old peace song that Mrs Stanton taught them in history class called 'We Shall Overcome.'

Matthew looks out at the girls and then turns

back and says, 'Let's just ignore them.'

'Ignoring the problem won't make it go away,' Mrs Martin says.

'My mother always says that, too.' Mark Ellison nods.

'My parents, too,' say a couple of the other kids.

'Everyone else's parents would let them ignore the girls.' Matthew is feeling desperate.

'Matthew. Let me list all the possible responses to that.' Mr Martin is smiling. 'Would we let you jump off the roof if everyone else's parents did? We're not everyone else's parents. As long as you are living under our roof, it doesn't matter what other people's parents say and, that old standby, No way José. Now did I miss any?'

'My father always says, "I brought you into this world. I can take you out",' Billy Kellerman offers.

Mr Martin says, 'So you see, Matthew, my son, you are going to have to deal with this problem. Think of your friends waiting for their ice cream and cake. Think of your dad waiting for his ice cream and cake. Think of how much better you're going to feel once you resolve this problem.'

Looking at the boys, then at his parents and then out the window at the girls, Matthew realises there's only one thing to do; actually, two, if you count moving to Disneyland, which his parents probably would not let him do. So there really is only one thing to do. Talk to the girls and work out some kind of truce.'

'Okay, I'll talk to them,' Matthew says softly.

'Terrific. I'll get a pillowcase, tie it to a stick and go out to the enemy camp to work out the arrangements. That's what they always do in movies and books.' Mr Martin heads out of the room.

'Honey. I don't think that's necessary.' Mrs Martin calls after him.

'It'll be fun,' he calls back.

Mrs Martin looks at Matthew and smiles. 'Your father. I married him because of his high sense of play. He sometimes drives me nuts with his high sense of play — and you take after him.'

Everyone watches as Mr Martin heads out of the door.

Everyone watches as Mr Martin goes over to the group of singing girls, sits down with them and talks.

The talk goes on for several minutes.

Finally, Mr Martin returns and says to Matthew, 'Here's the deal. You are very lucky, young man, that you have a lawyer for a father. This is what I have negotiated. The girls will come inside. You will apologise for all the things that you did that led to the formation of G.E.T. H.I.M., and I want that apology to sound sincere.'

'Okay.' Matthew stares at the floor.

'And,' Mr Martin continues, 'the girls have agreed, if your apology sounds sincere, to apologise for all the things that led to the formation of G.E.T. T.H.E.M.'

'Okay.' That word sounds a lot happier this time when Matthew says it.

'And,' Mr Martin says, 'the last part of the negotiations involved the kind of cake to be served. One of the demands is that there be no carob icing, just mocha, and that the cake be filled with butterscotch custard. That was their final demand. I gave in to it in the cause of furthering trust and understanding.'

'Huh.' Mrs Martin puts her hands on her hips. 'There's something fishy going on here. *That* is your favourite cake.'

'Not fishy — cakey.' Mr Matthew puts his hand on his son's head. 'What say we wrap up the apology session and I'll make the supreme sacrifice and run over to the supermarket and get the cake.'

Matthew smiles at his father, realising that his trouble is almost over. 'It's a deal.'

CHAPTER 18

'First you had to eat crow, then you got to eat cake.' Mr Martin pats his son's back.

'Huh?' Matthew looks up at his father.

'Eating crow is a phrase that means you had to say you were sorry in such a way that it seemed like a major punishment.' Sounding like a teacher, Mr Martin reaches for his third piece of cake.

'It would have been easier to eat a crow than to look at Vanessa acting like such a big shot winner.' Matthew runs his finger around the paper at the edge of the cake to get the icing.

The male Martins are in the kitchen alone, while the party is going on in the living room.

Mrs Martin is hiding out in her bedroom reading a book and worrying about the health of her family.

'Actually, things turned out all right,' Mr Martin says. 'The girls did apologise too. Although I do think that Vanessa saying, "I'm sorry that it was necessary to do all those things to you," was not the best apology in the world. But look at the bright side, there's a truce and you are the host of the first sixth grade girl-boy party. And you are a year older.'

'And I got lots of great presents.' Matthew grins.

Mr Martin grins back. 'You really did. Do you think I could borrow the suction cup bullet holes and one of the capsules of make believe blood? I'd like to wear them to work on Monday.'

'Absolutely.' Matthew nods.

'Thanks, kid.' Mr Martin wipes his face off. 'Are all the crumbs gone? I don't want any evidence when I go back to the room. Otherwise your mom is going to say . . .'

Both male Martins, in unison, say, 'Lips that touch sugar won't touch mine.'

Matthew heads into the living room.

The compact disc player is on, loud.

Most of the girls are standing on one side of the room. The boys on the other.

Walking up to Matthew, Vanessa Singer points at him and whispers, 'Listen, doofball. No more silly stuff or the girls of GET HIM will activate Plan B.'

Matthew debates doing something really gross, like another SBD or belching out a chorus of 'Happy Birthday.' Instead, he clutches his heart and pretends to writhe in pain. 'Oh, no. Not Plan B. Anything but Plan B.'

Sticking his tongue out, he crosses his eyes and sinks to the floor, muttering, 'Help. She's picking on me. What's Plan B?'

Vanessa looks down at him. Then she looks at everyone else looking at them and realizes that they know that she is the one who started it this time.

She sticks her nose up in the air and, after stepping over Matthew, says loudly, 'Just remember, a truce is a truce.'

Matthew jumps up and calls out, 'And a moose is a moose!'

Everyone laughs, except Vanessa.

Then Matthew goes over to Joshua and says, 'I guess there's no chance for the tournaments to finish.'

'I don't see why not.' Joshua cups his hands and calls out, 'Nintendo and Computer Tournaments are back on. Who else wants to join up?'

'Also we can drive the remote control car,' Tyler says, turning to Zoe, and smiles. 'Want to go for a ride with me?'

'But you don't have your licence,' Zoe frowns.

'It's a miniature car,' Lisa Levine tells her.

'And it's remote,' says Jil! Hudson, who thinks that Zoe is a little remote, too.

'Anywhere you want to go, I want to go too, Tyler,' says Zoe, sounding like syrup.

Ryma Browne pretends to stick her fingers in her mouth and makes little retching noises.

'Some day, when you two are more mature, you will understand what it's like to have a boyfriend.' Zoe makes a face at Jil! and Ryma.

'Trust me. I will never act the way you do around boys.' Ryma makes a face.

'My mother told me how to act, and she must be right. I have the boyfriend, not you.' Zoe looks like she owns the world.

Jil! debates asking if Zoe's mother knows so much about men, how come she has had four husbands, but Jil! decides not to.

Tyler looks a little embarrassed, but he also looks like he enjoys the attention. With four older brothers, he thinks he knows a lot about dating.

The tournaments begin.

Billy Kellerman wins at Nintendo.

His prize is a hand held game called Parachute.

Matthew wins at computer but, since it's his party, the prize goes to the second prize winner, Chloe Fulton.

'Good game,' Matthew says, glad that he had practised for a week before the party and extra glad that Chloe didn't know which game would be used in the tournament.

Chloe gets a set of science fiction books, which is terrific since she loves to read everything, especially science fiction.

'Can I borrow them when you're done?' Pablo Martinez asks.

'Absolutely.'

By the time the boy-girl part of the party is almost over, everyone is talking to everyone else. No one is fighting. Nobody is making a big deal out of it being a boy-girl party, except for Zoe, who keeps blowing into Tyler's ear because she heard that was a sexy thing to do. He keeps wiping the spit off, finally begging, 'Say it. Don't spray it.'

Jil! Hudson comes up to Matthew when he is standing alone by the bowl of gummy worms. 'I'm really sorry that I teased you so much about being boyfriend and girlfriend. I was just joking around.'

Matthew looks at Jil!, who is nervously chewing on the end of her hair.

He thinks about how much fun she can be when she isn't picking on him, how she's always thinking of fun things to do, how she's always so creative. He also thinks about Zoe's comment about how Jil! isn't mature enough to have a boyfriend.

'That's okay,' he grins. 'Some day when you're more grown up, maybe then we can be boyfriend and girlfriend. And if you really play your cards right, maybe we could be just like the Cleavers and live happily ever after.'

Then he picks up a gummy worm and puts it above his lip to form a moustache.

CHAPTER 19

Sunday.

All the boys have finally left after the sleepover.

Two were sick.

All of them watched as Danny and Amanda came back from their date.

All of them made kissing sounds with their lips on their hands when Danny started to kiss Amanda on the porch.

Amanda threatened to put all of them in the microwave, piece by piece and then she begged to be sent away to boarding school or to have Matthew sent to Reform School.

Matthew said it was not his fault.

Amanda disagreed.

The boys, at breakfast, ate ninety-four pancakes, spilled the syrup all over the flour, devoured three packets of vegetarian sausage without realising that it wasn't the real thing, drank two containers of orange juice and then held a belching contest.

Mrs Martin refused to award a prize to the winner of that competition.

'Thank goodness for paper plates,' Mr Martin says, throwing a bunch of them into the dustbin.

Trying to fit just one more glass into the dishwasher, Mrs Martin says, 'I didn't get any sleep last night with all of the laughing, did you?'

Mr Martin shakes his head.

'What did the boys want to talk to you about this morning? What was so private?' she asks, starting the dishwasher.

'They wanted me to judge the joke telling competition.' Mr Martin looks in the freezer to see if there is any ice cream left over for breakfast.

He can't find any.

'Who won?' Mrs Martin closes the freezer door before he can find out that she has hidden the ice cream container in the empty frozen spinach box. 'And what was the joke?'

'Patrick Ryan. And you don't want to know.' Mr Martin sits down at the table.

Matthew enters the kitchen very quietly, whispering, 'Is the coast clear? Did Amanda go over to Cindy's or is she hiding behind the refrigerator waiting for the chance to kill me?'

'She left an hour ago.' Mr Martin shakes his head. 'You know, you and the guys should not have used the computer to make up that sign, "Amanda Martin makes a Spectacle(s) out of herself." That wasn't very nice, and anyway, how did you know that glasses used to be called spectacles?'

'We studied Ben Franklin.' Matthew is glad that

119

he can show his parents that he actually remembers something from school.

There's silence at the table for a few minutes while Matthew waits to see if his parents are going to say anything else about how he's always tormenting Amanda.

Mr and Mrs Martin say nothing. They are so glad that there is peace and quiet again in their house.

'Mom.' Matthew breaks the silence. 'Dad. Do you realise that there are only three hundred and sixty-four days, eight hours and twenty-eight minutes until my next birthday?'

Mr and Mrs Martin look at each other as if they have been put in front of a firing squad.

Mrs Martin is the first to speak. 'Matthew Martin. Everyone else's children said they wouldn't bother their parents this morning. What do you have to say about that?'

Matthew grins. 'I'm not everyone else's child.'

'True.' Mr Martin looks at his son and realises that Matthew has the suction cup bullet holes on his arms. 'Very true.'

The looks that the parents give each other are unmistakable.

What will Matthew do next?

MAKE LIKE A
TREE AND LEAVE

MAKE LIKE A
TREE AND LEAVE

To Susan Haven and
Pamela Curtis Swallow

Acknowledgements

The Danzigers of Califon
Dr Steven Sugarman
Dr Mark Sherman
The Woodstock Conservancy

Chapter 1

'The suspense builds.' Mathew, holding up a baseball cap, looks at the three classmates who are sitting on his bedroom floor. 'Inside this very hat are four small, blank, folded pieces of paper. The fifth has an X on it. One of us and only one will get that X. Who, I ask you, who will get that paper?'

'If you'd cut out the drama and let us pick, we could answer that question very quickly.' Brian Bruno looks as if he's ready to grab the cap out of Matthew's hands.

Holding the cap behind his back, Matthew says, 'How can the suspense build if we pick right away?'

'I don't want suspense. I want to find out now,' Billy Kellerman says. 'Why do you always have to turn everything into a major production?'

'Because it's more fun that way.' Matthew grins. 'Anyway, Mrs Stanton made me the chairman of the Mummy Committee, so I get to do it my way.'

'Baloney,' Billy says. 'I overheard Mrs Stanton tell Ms Wagner that she only made you the chairman of the Mummy Committee because she's "trying to get you to use your leadership qualities in

1

a more positive way".'

'Baloney to you . . . I don't believe it.' Matthew glares.

'It's true. I was in the toilet in the nurse's office and the nurse had gone out for a minute, and the two of them came in and didn't know I was there. I also found out that Ms Wagner is going out with Mr King. You can learn a lot hanging out in the nurse's office.' Billy grins. 'And Ms Wagner told her about the time she made you the chairman of the fourth-grade Volcano Committee.'

'That explosion was NOT my fault!' Matthew protests.

'We only have two weeks to finish . . . We'd better get started,' Joshua Jackson reminds them. 'Come on, Matthew. Let's not start fighting and instead of letting the suspense build, let's build the mummy.'

'Oh, okay.' Matthew relents, holding out the baseball cap. 'Hurry up and pick, then. See if I care.'

Joshua closes his eyes and selects a piece of paper.

Billy Kellerman keeps his open and stares at the papers, wishing that he had X-ray vision, and then he chooses.

Brian Bruno crosses his fingers and then picks a piece of paper.

The paper falls to the ground because Brian Bruno is not good at holding on to paper with crossed fingers.

Matthew takes the last one out of the cap, puts the cap back on his head with the visor facing backwards, and says, 'At the count of three,

everyone open his paper... One... two...
three... go.'

Matthew looks down at his paper. There is no X.

He's not sure whether he's sad or happy... or
relieved.

There's no question that Joshua is happy. He's
waving his paper and yelling, 'No X. No X.'

For a minute Matthew thinks that he should have
put an L on the paper instead of an X so that Joshua
could have yelled out 'No L. No L,' since he's
acting like it's Christmas even though it's only
October.

Then he looks around.

Billy's smiling.

Brian says, 'How about if we make it the first
person who gets two X's? Isn't that a great idea?'

'Come on. It'll be fun. All we have to do is turn
you into a mummy like the Egyptians used to do,'
Matthew reminds him. 'It'll be easy. Billy got all the
stuff to do it from his father's supply cabinet. It
took the Egyptians seventy days to prepare a body.
We'll be done today.'

'The Egyptians only did it to dead people,' Brian
reminds him.

'Dead animals too.' Joshua has been doing a lot
of research.

'I'm still alive.' Brian gets up and starts pacing
around. 'I'm not a dead person. I'm not a dead
animal. I'm not sure that this is a good idea.'

'You thought it was a great idea until you got the
X.' Matthew gets up too. 'It'll be fun. We'll use the
plaster gauze stuff that Dr Kellerman uses all the

time on his patients. Remember, we used that stuff in third grade to make face masks.'

'That was just our faces. You're going to do it to my whole body. What if I get claustrophobia?' Brian looks less than overjoyed.

'Claustrophobia.' Matthew grins. 'Isn't that fear of a little old fat man in a red suit who shows up at Christmas?'

'That's so funny I forgot to laugh.' Brian scowls. 'You know that means fear of being closed in.'

'Look.' Billy starts taking out the boxes of plaster gauze that they've been storing at the bottom of Matthew's already messy closet. 'I'm planning to be an orthopaedist just like my dad and I've watched him work before. It'll be a breeze . . . and the plaster dries very quickly and then we'll cut it off of you. Nothing to it. Nothing at all.'

'And I'll teach you how to win at Super Gonzorga, that new computer game. You'll be able to beat everyone but me,' Matthew says.

'Everyone but you and Chloe Fulton,' Billy reminds him. 'You know she's almost as good as you are . . . sometimes she even beats you.'

Matthew chooses to ignore Billy. 'And Brian, I'll do the hieroglyphics poster with you. We'll do a poster about a guy named Hy Roglifics, who invents the Egyptian alphabet.'

'Let's not and say we did.' Brian shakes his head.

Joshua puts his hand on Brian's shoulder to stop him from pacing. 'I'll ask my father to make you the peanut butter cookies that you like so much.'

'It's a deal.' Brian smiles for the first time since

he's picked the X.

The boys hear a door slam downstairs as Amanda Martin enters the house.

'Matthew? Are you home, you little creepling?'

They also hear her yell again. 'Are you there, Barf Brain?'

Matthew helps Billy take out more boxes of plaster.

'Aren't you going to answer her?' Billy asks.

'Not when she calls me names. I bet that one of her dumb friends is with her. She always acts like a big shot when that happens.' Matthew makes a face. 'Maybe we should tie her up and put this stuff around her, but not leave the mouth, eye, and nose openings for her, and put her in the bottom of my closet for seventy days and use her for our school project.'

'Sisters.' Joshua says, knowing what it feels like to have an older sister, since he has one who is Amanda's best friend.

There's a pounding on Matthew's door, and Amanda flings the door open.

She's wearing a Hard Rock Café sweatshirt and a pair of old blue jeans. Blonde-haired, with blue eyes, Amanda squints as she glares at the boys, since she has given up wearing her glasses, except for when she absolutely needs to see. She is wearing at least one ring on each of her fingers, dozens of silver bangle bracelets on her right arm, and earrings. The one on the right side has stars and moons on it. The earring on her left earlobe is a heart that is engraved 'Amanda and Danny Forever.'

'Privacy!' Matthew yells, thinking that every time he looks at his sister, she seems to be getting much older . . . and much meaner.

'You didn't answer. I needed to know if you were here, since Mom and Dad said that I have to check on you. It's not my fault that they both work and I have to check.' She looks around the room at all the boxes. 'What are you guys planning to do . . . make face masks like they do in third grade? You'd better do it downstairs, on the back porch, so it doesn't make a mess. You know that our parents will kill you if you ruin the new wall-to-wall carpeting.'

Matthew realizes she's right but still doesn't answer.

Amanda stares at him. 'Cindy's with me and we're going to be upstairs in my room discussing private stuff. So don't bother me.'

Matthew is getting sick of the way that she acts towards him in front of his friends but knows that if he says something, it will get worse.

It's not fair that one kid gets to be older and the boss all the time.

Amanda leaves.

Matthew looks at his friends and says, 'Let's go downstairs and get as far away from that dweeb as possible.'

'And as close to the refrigerator as possible.' Joshua is getting hungry until he remembers how Mrs Martin believes in health food. 'Is there anything good in there . . . anything edible?'

Matthew grins widely, showing his dimples. 'My dad and I made a deal with her. We can have one box of stuff in the freezer and one thing in the refrigerator that she isn't allowed to complain about. We have a large bottle of soda and a box of frozen Milky Ways.'

'Great. Let's get these boxes downstairs and then do some serious snacking before we get to work,' Joshua suggests.

As the boys head down the steps carrying the plaster gauze, Matthew thinks about how this is going to be the best sixth-grade project ever. Mrs Stanton is NOT going to be sorry that she picked him to be chairman.

Chapter 2

Brian Bruno stands on the porch wondering why he didn't join the Pyramid Committee instead.

A giant dustbin bag with a hole in the middle for his head has been placed over his body so that only his feet, neck, and head show.

A bathing cap covers his ears and red hair.

Vaseline is smeared over his freckled face.

Joshua Jackson is holding a Milky Way bar to his mouth so that he can nibble on it.

'We're going to have to stop feeding you soon,' Matthew informs him. 'We're almost up to your chest area and what if you start to choke? We won't be able to do the Heimlich manoeuvre on you because you'll be all covered up with plaster.'

Matthew is trying to be the most responsible chairman of a Mummy Committee ever.

Continuing to wind the bandages around, while Billy wets the gauze so that it turns almost instantly into a plaster cast, Matthew says, 'Brian, how about letting us do some of the real stuff that the Egyptians used to do? We can cut a slit in the left side of your body and take out your liver, lungs, stomach, and intestines.'

'Forget it,' Brian mumbles, his mouth full of Milky Way.

Matthew does not care to forget it. 'Then we can embalm them and place them in a jar.'

'Cut it out.' Brian is getting very unamused.

'That's what I was just suggesting.' Matthew smiles and continues. 'Did you know that the Eyptians used to remove the brain through the nostrils, using metal hooks? That would be a cinch. I'd just have to look up in the attic for one of the hooks we used to use when we made pot holders. Don't you think that's a great idea?'

Brian looks like he does not think it's a great idea. He thinks that Matthew may not be the best head of the Mummy Committee of all time.

The other guys look at each other and think that it's time to change the subject.

Billy looks at the mummy/Brian and says, 'We should use the three-inch tape for his face, not the four-, five-, or six-.'

'Let's do another layer or two first on the rest of the body,' Matthew says. 'We have to make sure that it'll be strong enough not to break after we cut it off Brian, put the two sides back together, and plaster it together.'

'Fair deal.' Billy is really enjoying pretending to be a doctor.

As they work, Joshua holds up a glass of soda and a straw so that Brian can sip.

He keeps talking to Brian to help him keep his mind off what's happening. 'It's a shame that

Amanda and Cindy are so rotten that they'd never give us any old jewellery even if we asked them. Did you know that there should be magic amulets tucked between the wrappings? That would make it more accurate.'

Brian doesn't want a history lesson. 'Would you guys please hurry up? I'm beginning to have trouble standing here. This is getting heavy . . . and I think I'm going to have to go to the toilet soon.'

Joshua immediately puts the soda away.

'We're almost done.' Matthew starts putting the gauze on Brian's face, careful to leave large holes for his eyes, nose, and mouth. 'Billy, stop working on the body. Help me with Brian's face.'

As Billy starts working on the face, Joshua helps to prop up Brian.

Matthew goes for his mother's biggest pair of scissors.

He returns just as Billy is finishing.

It looks great.

'Get me out of here, you guys.' Brian's voice sounds a little muffled.

Checking, Matthew sees that Brian is getting enough air.

Looking, he can see how Brian just might be getting a little tired.

'No sweat,' Matthew says, to reassure him.

'Easy for you to say. You're not covered by a plastic dustbin bag and a ton of cement.' Brian does not sound happy.

Matthew sits down on the floor, ready to cut Brian out of the mummy cast.

It doesn't take him very long to realize that the scissors are not going to cut through the cast.

'Why don't *you* try this, Billy?' He hands the scissors over, trying to look and feel calm.

It takes Billy an equally short period to discover the limitations of the scissors. 'This always worked in third grade.'

'I don't think we had as many layers,' Matthew says softly, knowing that he is in deep trouble, deep deep deep trouble.

'What's going on out there?' Brian begins to sound panicky.

Matthew goes up to his mummy/friend and says, 'I don't know how to tell you this, but we've run into a minor problem.'

'My father's going to kill me if he finds out,' Billy says. 'I asked if I could take just a few rolls. He thought that we were making masks again.'

Joshua says, 'Someone give me a hand supporting this. He's getting heavy.'

Matthew makes a decision, one that he doesn't like but knows is necessary. 'I'll be right back. I'm going up to get Amanda.'

'Hurry,' everyone else says at once.

Rushing out of the room and racing up the steps, Matthew realizes that while Brian Bruno is in heavy-duty plaster, he, Matthew Martin, is in heavy-duty trouble.

And it's not going to be easy to get either of them out.

Chapter 3

Matthew knocks at the bedroom door, yelling, 'Amanda! Amanda! Open up.'

'What do you want? I told you not to bother me.' Her voice comes out loud and clear through the closed door.

Matthew opens it anyway.

Amanda and Cindy are sitting on the bed, using the machine that Amanda got for her birthday . . . the Crimper.

Their hair looks like it's been caught in a waffle iron. Cindy's is totally wrinkly. Amanda's is half-finished.

'I told you —' Amanda starts to scream.

'Emergency. It's an emergency. You've got to come immediately.' Matthew is almost out of breath. 'And you can't tell on me, promise.'

Amanda and Cindy jump off the bed.

As they run downstairs, Cindy remembers that the Crimper is still on and runs back up the stairs.

Matthew explains to Amanda as they rush into the kitchen.

Amanda looks at Joshua and Billy, who are

12

holding up the mummy and looking very scared.

The mummy doesn't look like it has much emotion, but it's obvious that Brian does.

He's yelling, 'Get me out of here. I want to go home.'

Amanda tries the scissors.

Cindy walks in and says, 'We've got an electric carving knife at home, but that would be too dangerous, right?'

'Right.' Amanda nods, knowing that she is going to have to be in charge of this situation and wishing this time that she were not the oldest.

'I'm calling Mom.' She picks up the phone and dials.

Asking for her mother, she listens for a minute and then says, 'Please have her call the second she gets back. Tell her it's an emergency . . . No . . . Everything is all right . . . sort of . . . but please have her call.'

Amanda informs everyone: 'One of the gorillas called in sick. Mom had to put on the costume and go deliver the message.'

Picking up the phone again and mumbling, 'I've begged her . . . absolutely begged her to get a normal job . . . but did she listen? . . . no . . . and she's even bought the company and has to spend more time there.'

'Hurry,' Matthew pleads. 'Do something.'

'I'm thirsty,' Brian says softly.

Rushing over to get the glass, Matthew realizes that the problem could get even worse . . . if that was possible to imagine.

Going back to Brian, he says, 'Which is worse? Thirst — or having to go to the toilet? Because if I give this to you ... you know what's going to have to happen sooner or later. You're going to have to go.'

Amanda is on the phone explaining the situation to her father. 'And hurry, Dad, hurry.'

Amanda hangs up and looks at Cindy as if to say, 'Do you believe this?'

Then she looks at Matthew.

'Don't say "I told you so," because you didn't,' he says. 'When's Dad coming home?'

'He's on his way immediately ... and he's going to call Dr Kellerman from the car phone to find out what we should do,' Amanda explains.

The boys look terrified.

All they wanted to do was make the best project.

'I can't stand up any more.' Brian sounds like he's going to cry. 'And I want to talk to my parents and I can't because they've gone away on a holiday and my grandmother's looking after us and she's going to have a heart attack if she finds out about this.'

Amanda walks over and pats the cast. 'Brian. It'll be all right. I promise you ... Just hang in there.'

'Where else am I going to go?' Brian asks and for some reason finds what she's said very funny and starts to laugh ... and laugh ... and laugh.

'Hysteria,' Amanda, who has been reading psychology magazines, thinks. What should I do? ... Should I do what they always do in the pictures? ... slap him and say, 'Get a hold of yourself'? But how can that help? ... I'd only be hitting the cast . . . and breaking one of my nails . . . and how *can* he get a hold of himself? . . . He's in a full-length body cast.

Amanda is beginning to feel a little hysterical herself.

Mr Martin rushes into the house and looks at the situation. 'Okay. Everyone stay calm. I've talked with Dr Kellerman and here are the possibilities.'

'I want to go home.' Brian has stopped laughing and is very upset. 'I want to get out of here.'

'Okay. I promise that we will get you out of there as quickly as possible, in the best way possible.' Mr Martin looks over at the scissors and quickly realizes that they are not going to work. 'Dr Kellerman says that we can put you in a warm tub of water and the cast will become soft enough to take off in about half an hour.'

'He won't fit into the bathtub. He's too tall and standing too straight.' Amanda is calming down, now that she is not the oldest person in the room.

'Then we're going to have to get you over to Dr Kellerman's right away,' Mr Martin decides. 'But he won't fit into my car. . . . We just may have to call an ambulance.'

Brian starts to cry.

Actually no one in the room is feeling very good either.

There's a moment of silence, and then as Mr Martin picks up the phone to call the emergency number, Mrs Martin rushes in, wearing the gorilla costume.

'I just stopped by on my way back to work to see

15

if you needed anything and . . .' She looks at everyone. 'What's going on?'

Quickly Mr Martin explains.

Mrs Martin says, 'Amanda. Cindy. Come with me. I want you to help me empty out the station wagon. Amanda. First, though, I want you to put your glasses back on. You know that you must wear them.'

As the females rush out, Mr Martin says, 'Brian. Everything's going to be all right. I'll be back in a minute. I'm going to get something out of the garage.'

'Don't leave us alone.' Billy is afraid that he's getting too tired to help keep Brian from falling.

'Just for a minute.' Mr Martin rushes out, returning in a few minutes with a piece of equipment that is used to move heavy things. 'I just remembered this dolly. We haven't used it in years.'

Mrs Martin and the girls return.

Mr Martin continues, 'Honey. I want you to help the boys support Brian while he hops onto this dolly.'

It takes a few minutes but finally Brian is on the dolly, and Mrs Martin and the kids make sure that he stays on while Mr Martin wheels the dolly over to the car.

Mrs Martin works her way into the front of the back section of the station wagon. It is not an easy task for a person wearing a gorilla suit, but there is no time to change.

Everyone helps lift and slide Brian into the back section of the car.

16

'I want someone to hold my hand,' he cries out.

'I'll get in and pat on the cast.' Amanda crawls into the back, her hated glasses back on her face. 'Cindy, could you wait here until we get back? If Danny calls, don't tell him about this. I want to . . . later.'

'Okay.' Cindy nods.

'I'll drive this car,' Mrs Martin says. 'Honey, you take your car.'

'I want to go. Please,' Matthew pleads. 'I want to help.'

Mrs Martin quickly says, 'Billy. Matthew. You come with me. Joshua and Cindy, would you please put this stuff in the garage?'

She points to some of the things that are used by her message-delivery company . . . a chicken suit, boxes of balloons, Mouse outfits, confetti, and heart-shaped boxes.

'Sure.' The Jacksons immediately get to work.

Mrs Martin talks quickly. 'Just let your mother know what's going on. And we'll call Brian's family as soon as we get to the doctor's.'

While they're driving along, Matthew looks at his mother, who has taken the gorilla head off but is still wearing the gorilla body. 'Mom, I'm sorry. We didn't mean to do anything wrong. I promise. Is Brian going to be all right?'

Mrs Martin nods. 'I think so. Just stay calm. We'll discuss this later. The important thing right now is to get him out of there and never do anything like this again.'

'I promise.' Matthew sits quietly for the rest of

the drive.

Amanda also sits quietly, hoping that no one she knows sees them. A mother in a gorilla suit and her own half-crimped hair are just too embarrassing for words.

Billy Kellerman sits in the back seat wondering what his father is going to do. He knows what he's going to do to *Brian* . . . help him. . . . He's not so sure what his father is going to do to him, his son.

Everyone gets to the office at the same time. Dr Kellerman is waiting at the door with a stretcher. He and his nurses and the Martins, as well as some of the relatives of waiting patients, lift Brian onto the stretcher and get him into the office.

Once Brian is on the examining table, everyone except the medical staff and Mr and Mrs Martin goes back into the waiting room.

Matthew and Billy explain to everyone how it was all a mistake, how they were just trying to do the best sixth-grade project, that they had no idea that it would all end like this, that they hope that Brian is going to be okay.

'He'll be fine, boys. Don't worry.' An older woman tries to comfort them. 'Dr Kellerman is a wonderful doctor.'

Her husband looks at Amanda and says, 'Is she also part of your Egypt unit, or did she just stick her hand in an electric socket?'

Amanda puts one hand up to her half-crimped hair, puts her other hand over her face, and tries to think of the best way to get back at Matthew.

'Don't listen to him,' the old woman says. 'My

husband is quite a kidder. He just likes to joke around.'

Amanda is all ready to say, 'Yeah. He's about as funny as a rubber crutch,' until she remembers where she is, in an orthopaedic doctor's office. She says nothing.

The old man continues, 'I guess your little mummy friend is all wrapped up in his problems. . . . But don't worry . . . there's really no gauze for concern. . . . Get it? No *gauze* for concern.'

'Melvin, that's enough.' His wife pats him on the hand. 'Remember, there is a little boy in the office who needs help. This is not the time for your corny jokes.'

Everyone in the office quietens down and thinks about Brian, who is at that moment being talked to by Dr Kellerman.

'Brian, there is nothing to worry about. In a little while we will have you out of there.' Dr Kellerman speaks softly, calming down not only Brian but also Mr and Mrs Martin, who are standing nearby.

In a very muffled voice, Brian says something.

Leaning over, Dr Kellerman asks him to repeat it and then tells the Martins, 'Brian says that as long as it's gone this far, I should try to save the cast so that they can still use it for the mummy project.'

'What a guy.' Mr Martin pats the cast. 'Brian, don't worry. We'll do whatever is best for YOU.'

'What is best?' he asks the doctor.

Dr Kellerman smiles. 'We can do both. Get him out quickly and save the cast.'

19

Leaning over, he explains. 'Okay, Brian. I'm going to use the cast cutter. Don't worry. I know that it looks like a pizza cutter and sounds like a buzz saw . . . but it's not. It'll be a little noisy because attached to the saw is a vacuum cleaner, which sucks up the dust from the cut cast. Brian, don't worry. The saw doesn't even turn round and round. It vibrates quickly. First I'm going to take the face mask off to give you more breathing room and then I'll take off the rest.'

The Martins stand there and watch the doctor work.

Dr Kellerman cuts through the plaster around Brian's face, uses a cast spreader, and then lifts off the face mask.

Everyone looks down at Brian's face, which is all scrunched up and covered with dust.

As Dr Kellerman brushes off the dust, he says, 'See, I told you it would get better. How are you feeling?'

Brian nods. 'Better. But I need a pee . . . soon.'

Dr Kellerman continues working.

Mrs Martin strokes Brian's face and talks to him.

Dr Kellerman and his nurse lift the front of the cast off.

Taking it, Mr Martin leans it against the wall.

The doctor asks the nurse for a pair of scissors.

'No.' Brian yells. 'Don't cut me. You promised.'

'I'm going to cut the garbage bag off,' Dr Kellerman explains. 'It's not good for you to be in it, and it's covered with plaster.'

'But I only have underpants on under this.' Brian

looks up at everyone.

'I'll loan you one of my doctor jackets,' Dr Kellerman says. 'Now, let's get you up and out of there.'

Mr Martin and Dr Kellerman help Brian sit up.

Brian looks at Mrs Martin. 'You're dressed like a gorilla.' And then he starts laughing.

Everyone begins to laugh.

Dr Kellerman and Mr Martin help Brian get out of the plastic bag.

The nurse and Mrs Martin look the other way, since that was the only way that Brian would agree to get out of the garbage bag.

Then Mr Martin helps Brian to rush to the toilet.

When they come back, Dr Kellerman gives Brian an examination to make sure that everything is okay.

It is, and Brian stands up to get a hug from Mrs Martin.

Brian, dressed in a doctor's coat that is about five times too large for him, gets a hug from Mrs Martin, dressed in her gorilla suit.

Dr Kellerman takes a Polaroid picture and then looks at Mr Martin. 'I believe that there are several young men in my waiting room, one related to you, one related to me. Something tells me that these young men should have a talking to.'

'I agree,' Mr Martin nods.

'I'll take Brian to his house and meet you at home soon,' Mrs Martin says and leads Brian out into the waiting room, where all the waiting patients, their families, their friends, and Amanda applaud the release of Brian from his plaster prison.

The two people cheering the most are extremely happy, even though they know that they are due for the lecture of their young lifetimes.

Nurse Payne sticks her head out the door. 'William. Matthew. Please come in. The doctor and Mr Martin will see you now.'

Chapter 4

'Timber!' Matthew yells as the plaster mummy almost falls to the classroom floor.

Mrs Stanton helps to prop it up against the back wall and says, 'Boys, be careful. You worked very hard on this project and I would hate anything to happen to this mummy.'

Pablo Martinez says, 'Yeah. Especially since Brian was so *into* the project.'

'I understand that after his performance as Mummy Dearest, when Brian got out . . . there was a cast party.' Tyler White starts to laugh.

The Mummy Committee pretends to ignore all the kidding.

Mrs Stanton makes sure that the mummy will stand on its own and says, 'Enough joking around. This is an excellent project. Now, everyone get ready. In a few minutes Egyptian Feast day is going to begin.'

Everyone starts rushing. Some of the students finish setting up projects. Others are getting costumed.

Visitors start to arrive: parents, Mrs Morgan, the

principal . . . Mr Peters, the vice principal, the media specialist, Ms Klein, who is carrying a video camera and is ready to immortalize the day on film, Mrs May Nichols, who is the seventy-eight-year-old who lives on the farm right next to the school.

Matthew comes running up to her. 'Hi, Mrs Nichols. Long time no see. Did you have fun on your trip? Did you bring me anything? Got any of those great chocolate chip cookies on you?'

Mrs Nichols smiles at Matthew, who is one of her all-time favourite people. 'Yes, I had fun on my trip. I brought back some wonderful stories about some of the great places I visited . . . and oh, yes . . . I know how you all feel about my cookies, and since it's been almost a year since I've been here, I baked a huge batch of them.'

She goes into her knapsack and pulls out a huge tin of cookies. 'I don't think that this is Egyptian, but I know how much you all like these.'

Everyone rushes over.

Matthew, who is there first, stuffs two cookies into his mouth at once and pockets three more.

'Piggard.' Vanessa Singer turns up her nose at him.

Matthew acts like he's whistling and sprays some cookie crumbs on Vanessa.

Mrs Nichols wipes the crumbs off Vanessa and softly says, 'Matthew, I think that you owe Vanessa an apology.'

Matthew remembers the time Vanessa started a club called G.E.T.H.I.M., Girls Eager to Halt Immature Matthew, and how everyone made him give in when the group picketed his birthday party. An apology is not what he wants to give Vanessa. Cow chip cookies is what he would like to give her.

'Matthew,' Mrs Nichols repeats, 'you got cookie crumbs all over Vanessa.'

Grinning at her, Matthew smiles and shows his dimples.

'Dweeble.' Vanessa glares at him.

'Matthew. An apology is in order, and Vanessa, dear, no name-calling.' Mrs Nichols thinks about how much she has missed seeing the sixth-graders, for whom she has been classroom volunteer since they were in kindergarten.

Matthew wants to please Mrs Nichols, so he shrugs, crosses his fingers behind his back, and looks at Vanessa.

'I'm sorry.' Matthew wants to add, 'I'm sorry that you exist in non-bug-like form.'

'Vanessa, aren't you going to accept his apology?' Mrs Nichols tests her luck.

'Oh, okay.' Vanessa wants to make Mrs Nichols happy too. 'Matthew, I forgive you . . . this time.'

Walking away, she thinks, But I'm not sure that I can ever forgive your mother for giving birth to you.

Mrs Nichols smiles at the children and wonders what her own child would have been like if he hadn't died of polio when he was three. Even though it happened over fifty-five years ago, she still thinks about it sometimes.

Matthew grins at her. 'You going to go sledging with us this winter again?'

Mrs Nichols remembers last time she went with Matthew and how they ended up in a huge snowdrift and she laughs. Somehow things are always fun when Matthew is around. She also remembers how much her 'old bones' hurt after that and she says, 'Maybe. But even if I don't, you can still sledge on my property, and I promise to make hot chocolate and cookies for all of you.'

'And you can always come to our parties.' Mrs Stanton pats her on her shoulder. 'You are the best classroom volunteer I've ever had.'

Matthew waves to Mrs Nichols, pockets two more cookies, and goes over to the area where some of the students are still setting up their projects.

There's the Egyptian house made by Chloe Fulton.

Matthew looks closely at the figures and yells, 'I didn't know that Barbie and Ken lived in early Egypt.'

The girls choose to ignore Matthew and continue with their own conversation.

'Egyptian Feast Day . . . It's finally here and it's going to be "so fun!"' Jil! Hudson jumps up and down in the classroom. 'Everyone is all dressed up . . . well, actually just all the girls . . . not the boys, since they refused to wear kilts . . . But we girls look great . . . and so do the projects . . . and the food . . . and it's just so terrific.'

Jil!, who changed the second *l* in her first name to an exclamation mark because she wanted more excitement in her life, loves it when Mrs Stanton has a learning celebration at the end of a unit.

All the girls are putting the finishing touches on their costumes . . . the jewellery, the make-up.

'Mellow out a little, Jil!' Vanessa Singer says, as she looks in the mirror and applies a lot of eyeliner around her green eyes.

Since Vanessa's parents say she is too young to wear make-up every day, Vanessa loves to use it when it's 'legal' at school on costume days.

'How do I look?' Chloe asks. 'I couldn't find my sandals this morning. Do you think Egyptians wore Reebocks?'

Lisa Levine says, 'It's an anachronism.'

Chloe, who has no idea that *anachronism* means 'anything out of its proper historical time,' says, 'I prefer to think of it as a fashion statement myself. Sort of Style on the Nile . . . Chloepatra, queen of the Nile.'

Everyone groans and then Cathy Atwood sighs and fingers the wig on her head, which is from an old Raggedy Ann costume. 'Don't worry. You look terrific. I, however, look like a first-class jerk. The rest of you all have hair that was long enough to bead.'

Ryma Browne vigorously shakes her head from side to side, causing the rows of beaded hair to hit the back of her head and then the front of her face. 'Bead lash . . . Listen, you're so lucky, Cathy. You saw what it was like at last night's pyjama party. It took hours to plait and then bead our hair . . . and then some of us had trouble sleeping on it.'

Jessica Weeks laughs. 'I told you to wear tights on your head. That would keep it in place while you slept. But some of you wouldn't listen. I should know. My African ancestors used to cornrow and bead their hair all the time. And so did my mother when she was younger. So I know.'

Cathy giggles, remembering the scene at the party. 'You did look pretty silly with tights on your heads. Especially you, Sarah.'

'Well, no one told me to cut off the legs first.' Sarah Montgomery blushes.

Lisa Levine, who loves to study, speaks. 'Actually Cathy is more historically accurate than we are. Egyptian grown-ups wore wigs of flax. They shaved their real hair and polished their heads.'

All the girls say 'Yuck' at once.

Lisa continues, 'If we wanted to be even more historically accurate, we would put cones of scented fat on our heads, and then as the feast goes on, the scented grease would melt and run down our faces. That's what they used to do to stay cool.'

There is another chorus of 'Yuck.'

On the other side of the room Ms Klein is filming Pablo Martinez, who is holding onto his pet snakes, Boa'dwithSchool and Vindshield Viper, and explaining how the Egyptians used reptiles to get rid of vermin.

Matthew is standing in the background, making faces and hoping to get into the picture.

'Enough, Matthew.' Ms Klein lowers the video camera. 'I already took a picture of the Mummy Committee and their project.'

Trying his best to look innocent, Matthew says, 'I was just standing guard to make sure that the snakes didn't eat the class gerbils.'

'Enough, Matthew,' Ms Klein repeats.

Matthew grins. 'You know that in Egypt some of the snakes were called asps. In fact one of them bit Cleopatra and she died. I'm just hanging around here to make sure that Pablo doesn't spend so much time with his snakes that he turns into one himself. I wouldn't want him to make an asp out of himself.'

'That's more than enough, Matthew Martin.' Ms Klein is never sure what to do when Matthew is around, whether to laugh or give him detention.

Mrs Stanton claps her hands. 'All right. Everyone settle down. We're getting ready to play some games . . . Get ready for $100,000 Pyramid, Name that Sphinx, Pharaoh Feud, and Scribeble.'

Everyone quietens down.

Matthew looks across the room.

Mrs Morgan is writing down Mrs Nichols's chocolate chip cookie recipe.

Mrs Nichols is dictating the recipe and at the same time helping to adjust Jil! Hudson's sheet/dress, which is in danger of falling off.

Pablo is trying to get Mr Peters, the vice principal, to kiss a snake.

Matthew looks across at the mummy and thinks about how much Mrs Stanton likes it.

Looking at Vanessa Singer, he thinks about what kinds of things he can do to torment her.

Matthew is happy that the work part of the unit is over and the party is about to begin.

He wonders what the next major class project will be.

Chapter 5

'Popcorn time.' Mr Martin sticks his head into Matthew's bedroom. 'I'm taking a little break. Why don't you?'

Sitting on the floor of his bedroom wardrobe, Matthew feels like he's been saved, at least temporarily, from a fate worse than death — the dreaded closet clean-up.

Before his mother left to take Amanda to the eye doctor, she threatened to call the Board of Health and have his wardrobe quarantined if he didn't straighten it up and throw things out. More important, she threatened to take away television viewing for a week for every day that the job wasn't done.

The work has begun . . . and it's not a pretty sight. Things have been scattered all over the floor as Matthew throws them out of the wardrobe, not sure of where to put everything. There is his baseball card collection . . . four nerf balls . . . his remote-control car . . . a Yahtzee game with two dice missing . . . with three pieces gone . . . a broken ant farm with no ants . . . reams of wrinkled computer paper ... a pair of Superman pyjamas with an attached cape that Matthew hasn't worn since he was five but doesn't want to throw away ... and his collection of forty-two baseball caps, with slogans on them.

Matthew looks at the junk in his wardrobe that he hasn't even got to yet, and then he looks at the rubbish bin, where he is supposed to throw away a lot of things. So far the only things in there are notes from last year's teacher that he never gave to his parents, a used-up tube of Slime bubble gum, wrappers from junk food that he didn't want his mother to know about, two paper clips, and a used plaster.

It's definitely time for a break, he thinks. If his father can take a break from important law work he, too, can take a break from dumb old wardrobe cleaning.

'I'm coming.' Matthew stands up, hits his head on a wire hanger, and wonders if that's punishment for not finishing off first.

He also wonders if a wire hanger concussion would be just cause for getting out of cleaning a wardrobe.

He decides not to push his luck and mention it.

Joining his father, they go down the steps and head into the kitchen.

'It's terrific to have some time to spend together.' Mr Martin smiles, as he takes out the new Stir Crazy popcorn maker. 'Being a lawyer is not always easy. I've had to spend a lot of time on one of the cases, but I promise that it'll be over soon, and then we'll have some "quality time." '

Matthew grins, because he knows what fun he has when he is with his father, how his father can sometimes act like a kid.

Mr Martin takes out the oil and the jar of popcorn. 'I can't seem to find the directions. The only time we used it, your mother made it. Oh well, it can't be too hard to figure out. I'm going to put in two tablespoons of oil. Do you remember how much popcorn your mother used?'

Scrunching up his face, Matthew tries to concentrate on visualizing his mother at the popcorn maker. 'I think she used two cups.'

'Two cups it is, then.' Mr Martin fills the bottom of the machine, puts the plastic yellow dome on, and plugs it in.

They watch as the stirring rod pushes the kernels around. In a few minutes the dome beings to steam up and the popcorn starts to pop and jump up.

Just then the front-door bell rings and Matthew and his father go to check who is there.

It's the postman and he needs a signature in exchange for a large envelope.

Mr Martin signs, sees that it is business information, and says, 'I can hear that the machine is still popping. We shouldn't leave it unattended. Let's get back.'

They reach the kitchen at the same time and both stare at the popper in amazement.

The dome is practically up to the kitchen cabinet. Popcorn is exploding all over the place, coming out the sides.

'How come this didn't happen when Mom did it?' Matthew shakes his head and then starts to laugh.

Mr Martin also begins to laugh and quickly pulls out the plug.

He stares at the machine and tries to figure out how to turn the bowl over without spilling the popcorn that is above the Stir Crazy base and below the yellow dome bowl. There's obviously no way this is going to work.

Mr Martin attempts it anyway, snapping the yellow plastic cup over the bottom of the dome, being careful of escaping steam, and laughing as he turns over the bowl.

The bowl is filled with popcorn.

So are the worktops and the floor.

It looks as if the Martin kitchen has been bombarded with a popcorn blizzard.

There are crunching sounds as Mr Martin and Matthew walk across the room.

Matthew sticks his hand into the yellow bowl, grabs a handful of popcorn, and puts it in his mouth. 'It's a little dry, Dad.'

Looking at the floor, Mr Martin says, 'It's a little messy, Matthew. I think it's Broom Time.'

Matthew decides that this is probably not the perfect moment to ask his father why he forgot to melt the butter and instead gets a broom, which he hands to his father.

Sweeping, Mr Martin wonders how this happened, how he could manage to graduate from college with high honours, get through law school easily, pass the law boards with no problems, and not be able to make popcorn, at least not the correct way.

Matthew watches, continuing to eat the popcorn.

'Get the dustpan.' Mr Martin is beginning to think this is not as funny as he originally thought it was, because there is still popcorn all over the place.

'Hi, pop,' Matthew says, picking up a piece of the popcorn.

Mr Martin looks at the mess. 'Sometimes this family gets pretty corny.'

As they look at each other and laugh, in walk Mrs Martin and Amanda, who crunch on some of the popcorn.

'I'm afraid to ask.' Mrs Martin shakes her head.

'I don't suppose that you would consider taking over sweeping this up, would you?' Mr Martin asks, hopefully.

'No.' Mrs Martin sits down at the kitchen table. 'I don't think so.'

It was worth a try, Mr Martin thinks.

'This looks so gross. Let me guess.' Amanda takes a handful of popcorn. 'This is the work of my only brother . . . the incredible Matthew Martin.'

Matthew makes a face at his sister, folding his upper eyelids up, flaring his nostrils, and sticking his tongue out.

He figures it's safe to do, since she doesn't have her glasses on and she'll never see it.

'Mom, tell Matthew to stop making that disgusting face, that he'll be sorry . . . that one of these days his face is going to freeze like that.'

Amanda puts her hand on her hip.

It's a miracle, Matthew thinks. My sister has twenty-twenty vision, to go with the rest of her measurements, which are twenty-twenty-twenty.

Mrs Martin says, 'Would someone please explain what happened?'

'I just wanted some popcorn,' Mr Martin says.

'Well, you got your wish,' Mrs Martin teases.

'Here's the story.' Mr Martin gestures. 'I put in two tablespoons of vegetable oil.'

'Good start,' Mrs Martin tells him.

Nodding, Mr Martin continues. 'Then I couldn't find the directions.'

'They're in the silverware drawer,' Mrs Martin informs him.

'Oh, of course.' Mr Martin grins. 'I should have known ... the silverware drawer ... the perfect place ... Anyway, Matthew and I tried to figure out what was the correct amount of popcorn to put in ... He seemed to remember that you used two cups.'

Mrs Martin starts to laugh. 'He did see me put in two cups ... but I used a one-third cup measuring cup. I used two of them to have two thirds ... One tablespoon of oil takes one-third of a cup. Double it and it's two-thirds of a cup — not two cups. The popper is designed to make six quarts of popcorn. You made twelve quarts, using half the recommended amount of oil.'

Everyone starts to laugh, except for Amanda.

'Isn't anyone going to notice that I am NOT wearing glasses? That I FINALLY got my contact lenses.' Amanda, who had been pleading for the lenses, wants everyone to tell her how wonderful she looks.

Her father does.

Matthew says, 'This popcorn really is too dry. Can we melt some butter, please?'

Amanda ignores him. 'I'm so excited. Dr Sugarman says that this is a new type of lenses that will work for me.'

She looks so happy.

Mrs Martin says, 'I remember my first pair of contact lenses. I got them when I was older than you are, Amanda . . . and you'll never guess what happened.'

She looks a little embarrassed. 'Maybe I shouldn't tell this story.'

'Tell us, tell us,' everyone begs.

She debates it for a minute and then says, 'Oh, okay. I guess I'll tell you. One day, about a week after I got the lenses, I was making out with my boyfriend and he swallowed one of the lenses.'

'Oh, Mom. That's so gross.' Amanda makes a face.

'What did the contact lens taste like, Dad?' Matthew wants to know.

Mr Martin looks up as he empties the popcorn into the waste can. 'It wasn't me. I didn't know her then.'

Amanda and Matthew both look at their mother, who grins at them.

'It's really gross to think of your own mother making out with someone who isn't your father. It's gross enough to think of your parents making out with each other.' Amanda looks shocked. 'I think we should change the subject. Preferably back to me.'

Matthew says, 'I want to know who the other guy was so I can call him up and ask him what the contact lens tasted like.'

'I haven't seen him in years,' Mrs Martin tells him.

Just then the phone rings.

Mrs Martin gets up to answer it.

Matthew hopes it is his mother's long-gone boyfriend so that he can ask him about the lens.

Amanda hopes that it is her boyfriend, Danny.

Mr Martin, who hates talking on the phone, hopes it is for anyone else or that it's a wrong number.

It's obviously for Mrs Martin, since she calls no one else over to the phone.

It's a serious call. Everyone can tell by the expression on her face and the things that she is saying like 'Oh, no . . . When did it happen? Is she going to be all right? What can we do to help?'

She listens for a few minutes and then says, 'Let me know what's happening . . . what can we do.'

Hanging up, she turns to her family, who are sitting there very quietly.

'That was Dr Kellerman,' she informs them. 'He wants us to know that there's been an accident. Mrs Nichols has got hurt.'

Chapter 6

Mrs Stanton explains to the class, 'Over the weekend, on Saturday, Mrs Nichols got up on a ladder to change a light bulb and she fell off.'

Matthew thinks, I wish I'd gone over to her house to say hello. I could have changed the bulb and then she'd be okay.

Continuing, Mrs Stanton says, 'She broke her hip and couldn't get up. Luckily she has a neighbour who calls every day at a certain time, and when there was no answer, the neighbour came over, found her, and called an ambulance.'

'I was in an ambulance once,' Mark Ellison says. 'Did they use the siren?'

Everyone has heard a million times about how Mark's aunt works for the rescue squad and how she let him sit in the ambulance once and turn on the siren.

Billy Kellerman volunteers the information that he knows. 'The neighbour, Mrs Enright, called my dad. And he examined her ... and she's got a broken hip ... and he's going to fix it. At least he's going to try to fix it. He said it's not so easy when it's a seventy-eight-year-old hip. But he's going to try. And my dad is real good. So I guess it's going to be all right.'

Matthew informs everyone, 'And then they called my mother because she and Mrs Nichols have known each other for a long time and Mrs Nichols was going to work for my mother.'

'What was she going to do ... dress up in a chicken suit or something?' Tyler White asks, laughing.

'That's a really old chicken,' Mark Ellison says.

'Stop it,' Chloe yells out. 'You both are being really gross and disgusting. Mrs Nichols is really nice.'

The boys know that, but all they can think of is Mrs Nichols dressing up as a chicken or a gorilla and delivering messages for Mrs Martin's company.

Matthew explains. 'One of the things my mother's company does is deliver get-well messages and presents to sick people. Mrs Nichols was going to be a grandmother who brought over chicken soup and stuff.'

'In a chicken suit.' Mark can't stop laughing.

'Enough, Mark.' Mrs Stanton is not pleased.

'Did your mother send over another old lady with chicken soup to Mrs Nichols?' Zoe Alexander asks.

'No.' Matthew shakes his head. 'She and my dad went over to the hospital yesterday and brought her the soup, some get-well balloons, and my dad brought her candy and my mother brought her some granola bars.'

'Ugh.' The students have all tasted Mrs Martin's

granola bars.

Matthew does not mention that, when they went over, his father was wearing a dog costume and carrying a sign that said 'Hope things aren't too Ruff for you,', and his mother was dressed in the chicken suit.

Matthew also doesn't mention that he didn't go with them because he gets real nervous around hospitals and that Amanda refused to go because being with parents dressed that way was just 'too embarrassing for words.'

Mrs Stanton continues, 'It's not always easy when you get older. But I'm sure that everything that can possibly be done for Mrs Nichols will be done. You know, I think it would be very nice of all of you to write a note to her. She's been a wonderful class-room volunteer, and I know how much she likes all of you.'

David Cohen, who hates to write, says, 'Can't we just call her?'

Patrick Ryan, who doesn't like to write or to be on the phone, says, 'Can't we just ask Ms Klein to videotape us saying something?'

Ryma Browne, who hates to look at herself on videotape, says, 'Let's just write notes.'

Mrs Stanton says, 'It's not a good idea to call too much . . . and there are no videotape machines at the hospital . . . so I think that the best thing is cards . . . or you can use the tape recorder, too.'

David Cohen raises his hand. 'Is it okay if some of us work together?'

Nodding, Mrs Stanton says, 'Yes.'

David, Mark Ellison, and Patrick Ryan call out, 'All right!'

Cathy is sent to the media centre to pick up a tape recorder and tape.

Mrs Stanton hands out the supplies — paper, glue, markers, pens, pastels, and crayons.

There is some disagreement on what to say on the tape recording.

The boys want to make animal sounds into the tape recorder to 'entertain' Mrs Nichols.

Mark suggests holding a belching contest into the recorder and letting Mrs Nichols be the judge.

The girls like neither of those ideas.

Nor does Mrs Stanton.

Finally the recording group settles down and speaks into the tape recorder, saying hello, that they hope that she gets better.

Mark yells 'Hip, hip, hooray' into the recorder.

It's erased because everyone else thinks that's a mean thing to say to someone who has just broken her hip.

Everyone puts the finished letters on Mrs Stanton's desk and it's back to schoolwork.

Chapter 7

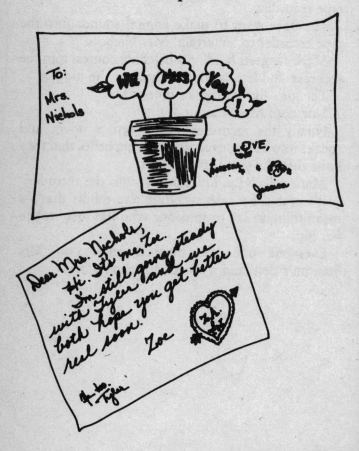

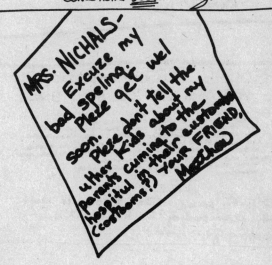

GET WELL SOON

I went over to your barn to feed Prince. (He's still the most <u>wonderful</u> horse in the world! Everyday I think about how great you were to sell him to me and let me keep him at the farm.) I told him about your accident. He looked <u>so</u> sad. So am I.

Come home <u>soon</u>.

LOVE,
Sarah

MRS. NICHALS'
Excuze my bad speling! Pleze get wel soon.

Pleze don't tell the uther kids about my parents cuming to the hospital about their awstonde (costooms?) Your FRIEND,
Matthew

43

FOR OUR FRIEND, MRS. NICHOLS,
What's the best time of the year......
Is it Jan? Feb? March? or April?
No !!!! It's **MAY**.

What's the best money.......
Is it quarters, pennies or dimes?
No !!!! IT'S **NICHOLS**.

MAY NICHOLS - SHE MAKES SENSE.
(cents- nickles, get it?)

GET WELL SOON

Ryma Cathy Katie

PERSONAL · PERSONAL · PERSONAL ·
FOR MRS. NICHOL'S EYES ONLY

PLEASE, OH PLEASE, OH PLEASE, GET BETTER SOON!
I MISS YOU SO MUCH EVEN THOUGH IT'S ONLY A FEW DAYS.
YOU HELP ME SO MUCH EVEN WHEN I FEEL REALLY BAD....
.... LIKE THE TIMES WE TALKED WHEN MY PARENTS GOT DIVORCED....
....WHEN MY DAD MOVED TO MONTANA.... WHEN MY GRANDMA DIED
AND YOU SAID YOU'D BE MY ADOPTED GRANDMA......
PLEASE DON'T LET ANYTHING BAD HAPPEN AGAIN.
I LOVE YOU.

LIZZIE
I wrote small so that no one else would
see this. I am sending this letter with a
magnifying glass. ♡♡♡♡♡

ROSES ARE RED
VIOLETS ARE BLUE.
MAYBE THEY CAN FIX YOUR HIP
with CRAZY GLUE!
HA. HA. JUST KIDDING.
signed, Yours Frank Dil

Dear Mrs. Nichols —
Sorry about how you broke your hip.
Are you going to have to wear a cast?
I also feel sorry for you because I personally don't know what it's like to wear one.
WARNING: Don't let the mummy committee near you.
Brian Bruno

Get We!! Soon Ji!!

45

Dear May,

Here are the kids' notes – also a tape. I haven't censored or corrected anything. I know how much you love the kids and I hope that this cheers you up.

Try not to worry.

I've been thinking about yesterday's phone call.

I know it's scary having something happen and having no family. Don't forget, though, that there are a lot of people in this town who really care about you – the kids you've helped (many who are now grownups), your friends, everyone at church.

Don't panic. Don't think the worst.

See you tomorrow   Suzanne
                      Stanton

Chapter 8

'Mom, dad.' Amanda bounds down the steps, yelling. 'You've got to give me permission to kill Matthew.'

Mr and Mrs Martin are sitting at the kitchen table.

'No. Permission denied.' Mrs Martin sips her herbal tea. 'And why are you dressed all in black?'

Amanda, who has on black shorts, a black tee-shirt, black tights, and black shoes, starts pacing back and forth. 'I have decided to try out different fashion looks, to find the "real me." But please don't change the subject. I want to know if I can rip Matthew into tiny little shreds and stuff the pieces down the toilet.'

'Absolutely not.' Mr Martin picks up his coffee cup. 'Plumbers are too expensive. I am, however, curious about what your brother has done this time to merit your homicidal rage.'

Amanda continues to pace back and forth.

'Everything. . . . If I tell you all of them, I'll be eighty years old before I'm done. He listens in on my phone conversations. . . . He imitates me. . . .

He's always threatening to blackmail me for something that I've never even done. . . . He "captures" the TV remote control and keeps changing MY shows to his stupid wrestling ones. He put washing-up detergent in my mouthwash. He told Danny that I have a very rare and highly communicable lip fungus. . . . And now today he's done the final thing. It's just the final straw, and he does it all the time.'

'If it's the final straw, how can he do it all the time?' Mr Martin looks at his daughter.

Amanda sighs. 'Don't try that lawyer logic on me. I know I'm right about this. That little creep never puts in a new roll of toilet paper when he's used up the old one . . . and then when I need it, absolutely need it, there's none there.'

Matthew, who has been outside the room, listening, walks in. 'That's right. Blame me. It's always my fault. How do you know I did it? Maybe it wasn't me. Boys don't always need toilet paper, you know.'

'Matthew. We really don't need a lesson in biology.' Mr Martin smiles and shakes his head.

Not finished with her rage, Amanda continues, 'Why do I have to share a bathroom with that creep?'

'I share a bathroom with your mother,' Mr Martin says. 'You don't hear us fighting.'

Actually Mr and Mrs Martin do argue about toilet paper. They just do it more quietly. Mrs Martin always puts it on the roller so that the paper rolls out from the bottom. Mr Martin always switches it around so that it rolls from the top. In fact he switches it around at houses where he is just visiting and at public lavatories too. Sometimes when the Martin parents disagree about something else, Mrs Martin reverses the paper just to get back at her husband. They do not, however, mention this squabble to their children, preferring to be good examples.

Amanda's pacing becomes even faster. 'I know he's responsible for not putting the toilet paper out. He never does . . . and he leaves the toothpaste spit in the sink . . . and he never puts the toilet seat down.'

'And she never leaves the toilet seat up. Also, she leaves all her dumb make-up all over the top and she spends hours hogging the bathroom.'

'Three bathrooms in the house and there's still all this fighting.' Mr Martin shakes his head. 'When I was a child, there was only one bathroom for four people. Of course the cat did have its own kitty litter pan.'

'Oh, Dad. Would you please take this more seriously? You never take my problems seriously.' Amanda begins a serious pout.

Matthew puts waffles into the toaster. 'The downstairs bathroom doesn't have a shower . . . and anyway, why do I have to be the one to run downstairs all the time? It isn't fair.'

Mrs Martin looks at her husband. 'Is this the way you want to be spending our day off? Listening to our children fight?'

He shakes his head. 'Enough. I want you kids to

stop this bickering. Whoever finishes the roll, put out another one. That's it.'

'And not just leave half a piece of paper on the roll so that you don't have to change the stupid roll.' Amanda glares at Matthew, who is busy filling each little square of his waffle with a drop of syrup.

Mr Martin shakes his head. 'Matthew, don't leave half a piece of paper on the stupid roll.'

Grinning, Matthew looks at his father. 'Tell her not to leave her stupid make-up all over the place.'

Mr Martin smiles at his daughter. 'Amanda, don't leave your stupid make-up all over the place.'

Amanda does not return the smile.

She turns to Matthew, who gives her his widest grin, then crosses his eyes, puts his finger up his nose, and sticks out his tongue.

Amanda sneers at him. 'Why don't you go to boarding school . . . or better yet, reform school. In fact why don't you do us all a big favour . . . MAKE LIKE A TREE AND LEAVE.'

Stomping off, she mumbles about how no one in the house understands her, how Matthew is such a big baby.

Matthew looks up at his parents and says, 'I guess she just made like a banana and split.'

Mr Martin laughs.

Mrs Martin just sighs and says, 'Matthew.'

Matthew sits down at the table and speaks in his most adult voice, one that he has been practising in the privacy of his own room. 'She really has turned into quite a pain, hasn't she? I just don't know what we are going to do with that child.'

His parents' mouths start to move into a smile, but they both stop before the smiles begin.

Matthew continues, 'Her attitude is rather awful, isn't it. Stamping around, talking to herself, hogging the telephone, putting on all that make-up, acting like such a big shot, treating a younger child so badly, accusing him of misuse of paper supplies. I do think that some form of punishment is in order. What do you think? . . . Taking away her telephone privileges, not letting her use eye make-up gunk for at least a week, sending her to reform school? . . . I ask you.'

Mr Martin looks at his son, who has just stuffed almost a whole waffle into his mouth and who has syrup running down his chin. 'Matthew. I want you to remember what Martin Luther King said: "We must live together as brothers or perish as fools." '

Nodding, Matthew tries to look wise and mature. 'I would be ever so happy to, Dad, but Amanda is my sister, not my brother.'

Mrs Martin sighs.

Mr Martin gets up to make himself some waffles.

Mrs Martin sighs again and wishes that they would eat what she is having, yogurt with granola.

Finishing the waffle, Matthew wipes up the left-over syrup with his finger.

'Matthew, stop that,' his mother says. 'So what are you planning to do today?'

'I'm meeting Joshua.'

'Where are you going?' Mrs Martin is one of those mothers who is most comfortable when she knows, at all times, where her kids are.

'Over to the clubhouse,' he tells her, referring to an area on Mrs Nichols's property, an old play house on her property that she has let the boys use since second grade.

Matthew's parents look at each other, and then his mother says, 'Enjoy it while you can. There's a rumour that Mrs Nichols is going to have to sell the property.'

Matthew can feel the waffles at the bottom of his stomach.

'And,' his father informs him, 'the contractor who wants to buy it is planning to put a housing development there, as well as a small shopping centre.'

Matthew feels like the waffles are going to make a return trip up and out.

Chapter 9

'We have to do something.' Vanessa Singer puts her hands on her hips. 'I've never heard of anything so disgusting in my entire life.'

For once Matthew and Vanessa agree on something.

Usually, when Vanessa uses the word *disgusting*, she is referring to Matthew.

This time, though, she is talking about the possibility that Mrs Nichols's property is going to be turned into a housing development and shopping mall.

'Maybe it won't be so bad. Maybe there will be some really great stores there. You know that there's no place around here to shop,' Zoe says.

Lisa Levine sighs. 'Zoe, sometimes you are so shallow . . . like a ditch.'

Zoe, who is standing next to her boyfriend, Tyler, and has her hand in his back pocket to show that they are a couple, says, 'Don't use language like that to me, Lisa Levine. We may not always agree, but I'd never call you a name like that.'

'D . . . ITCH . . . she said *Ditch*.' Jil! explains.

'Look, let's not fight with each other. Shake hands and make up. We've got to spend our time on more important things, like what we can do to save Mrs Nichols's property so that we have nature nearby, a place to go skating and sledging, a place that's really pretty. So, come on, you two, shake and make up.'

Matthew interrupts and begins to twitch. 'Shake. Shake. Shake.' And then he pretends to put on lipstick. 'Make-up. Make-up. Make-up.'

Vanessa glares at him and says, 'Disgusting,' and is not talking about the possible loss of property.

Lisa ignores Matthew, looks at Zoe, and smiles. 'Oh, okay.'

Zoe tries to take her hand out of Tyler's pocket but has a problem. Since she is wearing a large cubic zirconia ring on her left hand, it gets caught in Tyler's pocket, and when she turns her hand around, attempting to remove it, the ring scratches Tyler.

Finally her hand is freed.

She shakes Lisa's hand, while Tyler stands there wondering how badly his rear end has been scratched.

Vanessa continues. 'My parents said that some of the grownups are starting something called a conservancy to buy the land and save it for everyone's use . . . and that it's going to take a lot of fund-raising . . . that everyone is going to have to pitch in and help.'

Matthew pantomimes being a baseball player and says, 'Pitch. Pitch. Pitch. . . . And don't worry,

Zoe, I'm not referring to you.'

Even though Matthew really cares about saving the property, he can't seem to stop fooling around, especially when Vanessa is getting a lot of attention.

Vanessa tries to pretend that he is invisible. 'I think we should all do something to help earn the money . . . like a bake sale or a car wash.'

'Boring.' Matthew pretends to yawn. 'Boring.'

Vanessa no longer pretends he is invisible. 'Listen, twerp. My ideas are not boring. You are what is boring. You and the way you act. . . . You know how we could make a lot of money? We could charge you a nickel for every word that you misspell, a dime for every time you get detention. That way we could buy the land very fast. . . . We would probably have enough money left over to buy China, and I'm not talking about dishes.'

People laugh.

They think several things are funny. Matthew's spelling is one — *werm, sertain, nickle, alwaze, acetera*. Another funny thing is how Matthew can always get Vanessa angry, and then what happens next.

Matthew stares at Vanessa.

He does not like it when she mentions his bad spelling.

'Come up with something better.' Vanessa sneers at him.

'We could have a school fair and have a kissing booth and people would pay a lot of money not to have to kiss you,' he sneers back.

'We could have a Dunk The Doofus game and

55

you could be the Doofus.' She glares. 'Be serious, Matthew. Come up with something real. Or shut up.'

Now Matthew is really annoyed.

'I'm waiting.' Vanessa smirks.

A brainstorm hits Matthew.

So does a paper airplane thrown by his best friend, Joshua Jackson.

Matthew lobs the plane back to Joshua and speaks. 'Teams. We set up teams. You're the captain of one. I'm the captain of the other. Whoever raises the most money for the conservancy wins. You with your boring ideas. Me with my great ones. Deal?'

Vanessa looks at Matthew and then looks at the class.

She thinks, This is a good time to reassemble G.E.T.H.I.M., Girls Eager to Halt Immature Matthew, and says, 'It's a deal. G.E.T.H.I.M. against your team.'

Matthew thinks about the group that he wanted to start when the girls started their group and realizes that now is the time for G.E.T.T.H.E.M., Girls Easy to Torment Hopes Eager Matthew. Only this time the Second *T* won't be for Tormenting, but for TOTAL, as in *total* up more money, turn them into total wrecks.

Mrs Stanton walks into the classroom.

Joshua debates swallowing his paper aeroplane so that there is no evidence but instead quickly hides it in his back pocket.

Everyone in the classroom looks guilty, except

for Mrs Stanton, who looks a little annoyed.

She clutches her heart. 'Is this really *my* class of sixth-graders, the people who I told to take out books and read independently *at their desks*, while I answered a very important phone call? Can this really be my class, or have I stepped into an alternative time zone and found a class that looks like mine but is totally lacking in the ability or inclination to follow directions? Has an alien life-form invaded this room?'

Mrs Stanton's independent reading includes a lot of science fiction.

'Pay no attention to that woman behind the curtain,' Matthew says, thinking of the line from *The Wizard of Oz*.

'Detention, Mr Martin.' Mrs Stanton shakes her head at Matthew, who makes her laugh but also drives her nuts sometimes.

Matthew grins. Detention with Mrs Stanton will be much more fun than going home and having Amanda in charge.

'We're just talking about what it's going to be like if the woods by the school become a housing development and a shopping centre,' Lisa explains. 'Mrs Stanton — can't you do something to help us?'

'It's current events.' Pablo Martinez is sitting on top of his desk and swinging his legs back and forth. 'Aren't you always talking about how we should know what's going on in the world? How we should take stands on things?'

Mrs Stanton looks at her students. 'Everyone sit down. We will take some time to talk about this, but I have to make something perfectly clear. This situation is becoming a very big political issue in town, and as a teacher, I have to be fair and present both sides.'

'I bet you want more places to shop, too.' Zoe says.

Smiling, Mrs Stanton nods. 'It wouldn't be bad . . . not having to travel a half an hour away to buy clothes for my family. I'm just not sure that the Nichols property is the best place. There doesn't seem to be an easy solution.'

'What about all the animals?' Sarah sits down at her desk. 'What are they going to do . . . go to a store named Woods Are Us?'

'My mom says that the reason we moved here from the city was to get away from crime, to have fresh air, to be in a small town. A housing development is going to bring in more people, more cars, more pollution. That's what my mom says.' Mark Ellison shakes his head.

'Well, my dad says that it'll bring in more money for taxes to pay for more services and that it will provide more jobs for people . . . that you can't stand in the way of progress . . . that change isn't always such a bad thing,' Cathy Atwood calls out. 'I'm sick and tired of listening to everyone say bad things about the houses and the malls. My dad is the contractor.'

'Yuck.' Ryma Browne makes a face. 'How can your father even think of ruining that property, the place where we've all played since we were babies? I'm glad that my father doesn't have anything to do with trying to wreck everything. If my father did, I'd hate it. I'd rather have Freddy Kruger as my father, the *Nightmare on Elm Street* guy.'

Cathy looks like she's going to cry. She loves the property, too, but she also loves her father and knows that he's really a nice person.

'That really was not appropriate, Ryma.' Mrs Stanton shakes her head. 'Look, there are many sides to this issue, many things to consider. Mrs Nichols and her property have been part of my life since I was a little girl, so I understand how you feel. I can also see Mr Atwood's reasons for feeling the way that he does.'

'You were a little girl?' Matthew asks, grinning.

Mrs Stanton chooses to ignore his comment. 'I want each of you to think about why this is important to you and I want you all to consider both sides.'

'I don't care either way.' Patrick Ryan raises his hand. 'Because of my parents' divorce, my mom and I are going to move at the end of the school year anyway, so what's the difference to me?'

'That is an important point. There are obviously a lot of different reactions to this situation.' Mrs Stanton thinks for a minute. 'Instead of beginning our Greek civilization unit next, let's do our own Califon, New Jersey, unit. You will be part of it. I want you to go home and talk to your parents . . . or parent . . . or guardian . . . about your own roots, where your families come from . . . then I want you to do a family tree . . . tell about how your families came to Califon . . . and how you feel about the Nichols property and about what may happen to it. You can all take out a piece of paper and write down some of the questions you will ask your family. Any questions?'

'How long does this have to be?' Lizzie Doran asks.

'As long as it takes to be finished,' is the answer.

'Does spelling count?' Matthew wants to know.

Mrs Stanton nods.

Vanessa makes a little snorting sound.

Matthew continues, 'And you want us to ask our parents where we came from?'

Again Mrs Stanton nods.

Matthew grins. 'Last time I asked where I came from, they gave me a lecture about the birds and the bees.'

The glass giggles, all except for Vanessa Singer, who whispers, 'How immature' under her breath, and Mark Ellison, who practically falls off the chair laughing.

'Matthew.' Mrs Stanton uses her soft teacher voice. 'Enough already . . . I want everyone to get to work on this project right now.'

David Cohen raises his hand. 'Can we work together?'

Mrs Stanton shakes her head. 'It's a family tree. How can you work together unless you both come from the same family?'

'Someday,' Zoe announces, 'someday Tyler and I will be in the same family . . . and you'll all be invited to our wedding.'

Tyler blushes, and somewhere in the room

someone makes a retching noise.

'Get to work.' Mrs Stanton uses her stern teacher voice.

As the students take out their notebooks, their teacher smiles and thinks about how exciting this unit is going to be.

Matthew sits at his desk and thinks about how he would like to leave Amanda off the family tree and whether Vanessa is going to be drawing her family tree with a lot of apes swinging on it.

Chapter 10

'A pet wash. That sounds like a great idea.' Mr Martin looks up from writing a cheque to the conservancy. It is the first of three that they have pledged over a period of three years. 'I hope that you make a lot of money for the conservancy. It is a cause that your mother and I really believe in and it's wonderful that you and your classmates are helping.'

Matthew feels proud, but has one very important question about something that has been bothering him. 'Dad, what exactly is a conservancy?'

Mr Martin explains. 'You know that Mrs Nichols needs money and has to sell the land. You also know that a lot of people want to preserve the land and see that it's not commercially developed. In order for that to happen, all of the people who feel that way about the land have to donate money or come up with ways to get money.'

'Like an animal wash.' Matthew grins.

'Yes.' His father continues, 'If the money can be raised, the land will be preserved and watched over by the conservancy, which is a nonprofit group dedicated to saving places of special beauty and/or importance.'

Matthew wonders if the conservancy will ever want to save his house because it may some day be of historical importance because it's where he's grown up.

Mrs Martin walks over behind her husband and puts her hands on his shoulders. 'I just wish that Mrs Nichols was not in a position where she has to sell her land to take care of herself. That's a very sorry position to be in. She loves the place so much. When I visited her yesterday, she said that she wished that she were rich so that she could just stay there and eventually leave the land to the town.'

'That would be wonderful.' Mr Martin looks very thoughtful, the way that he often does when he's doing legal work. 'That really would be terrific. Mrs Nichols is so nice. How is she feeling?'

'Better.' Mrs Martin sits down at the table and puts unsweetened marmalade on her bran muffin. 'It's so sad. Remember how Mrs Nichols took that long trip last year and did all of the things that she always wanted to do . . . white-water rafting . . . a balloon ride . . . a mule caravan along the Grand Canyon . . . and she never got hurt? And then she comes back and falls off a stepladder in her own kitchen. How unlucky.'

Matthew looks down at his bran muffin and thinks how unlucky Mrs Nichols continues to be, that his mother brought a dozen bran muffins over to her at the hospital.

From upstairs comes the sound of Amanda

yelling. 'Don't anyone pick up the phone when it rings. It's for me.'

'Don't stay on too long,' Matthew yells back. 'I'm expecting a call from Brian about our animal wash.'

Mr Martin looks at his wife and son. 'Wasn't there a time when we actually saw Amanda's face . . . when there weren't just shrill orders coming out of her room? Tell me, Matthew, are you going to be like this when you become an adolescent?'

'No way, José.' Matthew grins, glad that for once he is not the bad one.

The telephone rings . . . and rings . . . and rings . . . and rings . . . and rings.

Matthew waits for Amanda to pick up the phone, hoping that it's really for him or there's a good chance that the line will be busy for hours, maybe even weeks.

'Enough. How do we know that it's not for one of us? How do we know that Amanda has not picked this moment to begin one of her endless bathroom marathons, doing who knows what to her hair?' Mr Martin picks up the phone. 'Hello. This is the Martin Home for the Chronically Bonzo. Head warden speaking.'

'Honey,' Mrs Martin sighs. 'What if that is someone from work? What if there is an emergency and someone needs to talk to me about a delivery? What if it is one of your clients?'

'It's not.' Mr Martin smiles and yells, 'Amanda. It's for you.'

Amanda rushes into the kitchen, sighing. 'Dad, I said not to answer it. Please. Doesn't anybody ever listen to me?'

'It rang eighteen times.' Mr Martin hands the phone to her.

'I can't find the receiver for my new cordless phone.' Amanda informs them. 'Cindy's just calling so that I can listen to the sound of the ring and locate the phone. I was getting really close to finding it and then *you* picked up the phone.'

Mr Martin hands her the phone.

'Cindy. Call me right back.' Amanda speaks into the receiver.

Mr Martin says, 'Make that five minutes. I want to talk to you.'

Sighing, Amanda says, 'Five minutes. . . . HE wants to talk to me.'

'*He.*' Mr Martin shrugs his shoulders. 'Now I'm *he*. Whatever happened to the good old days when I was Daddy? The daddy who could do no wrong, the *best daddy* in the whole wide world?'

'That changed just about the time I became *she*,' Mrs Martin informs him. 'I think it was about the time that "I hate my parents" hormone developed. In the psychology books I think it's called adolescence onset.'

Matthew adds, 'I think *he* and *she* is better than what she calls me: "Pukeface." '

Amanda puts down the phone. 'I don't think it's fair that you think this is all so funny. You act like it's a crime that I'm growing up, trying out new things . . . not being a dumb little kid who thinks her parents are perfect . . . and don't worry, Matthew, I never did think that you were perfect.'

Matthew pulls an imaginary knife out of his heart.

'We're just kidding around,' Mr Martin says, trying to be reasonable. 'Why are you so serious about everything? So sensitive. Can't you take a joke? And can't you stop tying up the telephone lines, the *family* telephone lines?'

Matthew thinks about how sometimes, especially in the old days, Amanda could be so nice and now that she's in eighth grade, she's so different. Maybe he should write a book about it and illustrate it. The book title could be *I Didn't Ask for Her to Be Born*, subtitled *She Couldn't Be Stopped*.

'It's not as if I didn't ask you not to pick up the phone. I did ask and you picked it up anyway.' Amanda feels justified in her annoyance.

'If it were more organized in there, you'd be able to find it.' Mrs Martin gives her daily commercial for neatness.

The phone rings again.

Amanda looks at her parents. 'Please. Let me go upstairs and find the receiver. It should only take a few seconds.'

They nod.

As Amanda rushes upstairs, Matthew speaks, using the grown-up voice. 'I really do think that you let that child get away with murder. I know that she bought the cordless with her own money, but don't you think that you should encourage her sense of sharing? Especially with her younger brother, who is often inconvenienced by not being able to get his own phone calls because she is always on the phone.'

The aforementioned phone stops ringing.

Amanda yells down the stairs, 'It's for you, Pukeface.'

'I'm going up to talk to her,' Mrs Martin says.

Mr Martin nods.

Matthew says, 'Talk is cheap. How about torture?'

His father picks up the receiver and hands it to Matthew.

It's Brian, asking him to come over to the house a few minutes early to help set up.

'I'm not sure if I can.' Matthew thinks about how messy it's going to be.

Brian says, 'My mother's making double-fudge brownies and said that if you get here soon, we can lick the bowl and the mixing spoon.'

'I'll be there in three minutes,' Matthew decides. 'Tell her that she doesn't even have to bother baking them, that the batter is best.'

As Matthew rushes out of the house, he hopes that the boys of G.E.T.T.H.E.M. make more money today than the girls of G.E.T.H.I.M.

He also hopes that Mrs Bruno is making a very large batch of double-fudge brownies.

What can go wrong on a day with brownies only a few minutes away?

Chapter 11

'Wash basins. Hose. Soap. Perfume. Mouthwash.' Brian points out the things that are ready.

'Perfume. Mouthwash.' Matthew's mouth is filled with brownies. 'What do we need those for?'

'To make the animals smell good ... doggy breath ... C.O. ... D.O. ... stuff like that.' Brian shoves a brownie into his mouth.

'C.O.? D.O.?' Matthew picks up another brownie.

'It's like B.O., but it's cat odour ... dog odour. ...' Brian grins. 'I made it up.'

Brian's seven year-old sister, Fritzie, comes out.

Matthew backs up, remembering how when Fritzie was little, she used to bite everyone. Even though she no longer does, everyone is still very careful around her.

'When will the animals get here? I want to watch.' Fritzie, who thinks she's very funny, purrs and then barks.

Brian, clearly embarrassed by his little sister but sure that his parents will not lock her in the cupboard as he requested, says, 'Don't worry. Her bark is *now* worse than her bite.'

Matthew is relieved, but continues to back up.

Fritzie takes a brownie.

Matthew moves forward and takes another brownie, thinking that he's more worried about a Fritzie bite than about getting bitten by one of the dogs or cats that the boys are planning to wash.

Joshua Jackson arrives with a huge board. 'My father cut this out for us and he gave us the spray paint to do the sign. I'll do the writing part, so that the spelling is correct, and Matthew, you can do the drawing.'

While the two best friends work on the sign, the rest of the boys arrive.

'Where's Tyler?' Patrick looks around.

'He helped put up the posters all over town,' Billy informs them. 'And now he's at his house.'

'Didn't Zoe let him off his leash?' Matthew looks up from the picture he is painting.

'He's allergic,' Billy says. 'Whenever he gets around dogs and cats, he sneezes and wheezes.'

'Sneezes and wheezes.' Matthew laughs. 'I wonder how he can go out with Zoe. She's the only kid I know with a mink coat.'

'A mink coat!' Fritzie gasps. 'That's like wearing a pet on your body. That's gross.'

'Go away, Fritzie.' Brian glares at her.

Putting her hand on her hip, she says, 'Make me. I'll tell Mommy that you're being mean to me.'

Brian continues to glare at her but he does nothing. His parents have already warned him that he is to 'let her have fun too . . . not be mean . . .

she's only a little girl.' Brian feels like there is no way to win with Fritzie, that maybe some day he'll get lucky and a huge tornado will lift her and take her to Juneau, Alaska, where the tornado will drop her in the middle of a very cold glacier. Until then Brian knows he's stuck with her.

'A mink coat,' Fritzie repeats. 'Did she give it a name like Spot?'

'She got it from her father. It was a "guilt gift," ' Patrick says. 'When her parents got a divorce, he gave it to her because he left the family . . . At least she gets something . . . My parents, when they split, didn't feel guilty and give me stuff . . . They said it was the best thing for everyone . . . I think I should have got a Porsche.'

'Does Zoe wear the coat to school?' Fritzie licks brownie off her fingers. 'And what do you want a porch for?'

'Fritzie. Please. Would you just go play in traffic.' Brian scowls at his sister.

'She wears it for special occasions,' Patrick says. 'Look, Fritzie. What if we bribe you to go away?'

Fritzie grins at Patrick, who is her favourite of all her brother's friends, even though she once bit him so badly that his ankle still has a scar.

She shakes her head.

'Okay. Everyone just ignore her. Pretend that she's not there,' Brian instructs.

'How does the sign look?' Matthew holds it up. It says, 'Paws for the Animal Wash.'

'Great.' Fritzie dances in front of it.

Everyone pretends she's not there.

While the sign is placed in front of the house, a station wagon pulls up, and out comes a woman, who takes out a German shepherd.

Not just any German shepherd, but a very smelly one.

'Skunk time.' Fritzie holds her nose. '*Adiós, amigos.*'

As she goes into the house, she takes the plate of brownies.

The woman says, 'We heard something in our garage and let Puppy go outside to see what it was.'

'Puppy!' Billy shakes his head. 'That dog must weigh two hundred pounds.'

'Two hundred very smelly pounds.' Matthew holds his nose.

The woman nods. 'I know. Not only was our dog sprayed. So was our car. I was so glad that my husband remembered seeing your sign on the telephone post by our house.'

Everyone wishes that Tyler had missed going to the lady's block.

She starts pulling cans of tomato juice out of the back of the car.

'Washing the dog in this will help get rid of the smell.' She smiles at the boys, who don't smile back. 'Look, boys, I know that the money that you earn is going to the conservancy. My husband and I were going to make a donation to it anyway. We'll give you the cheque and it can be part of what you earned ... And we'll get Puppy cleaned. It's actually a good deal for everyone.'

The dog walks over to Matthew and licks his

hand.

Puppy's owner hands him the cheque.

Looking at it, Matthew sees the amount.

'That's what we were planning on giving,' she says. 'So how about it?'

'It's one hundred bucks, guys.' Matthew tells everyone. 'Think about how many cars the girls are going to have to wash today to get that much, and this is just our first job of the day.' Joshua whistles. 'One hundred dollars.'

'The conservancy is a good cause. When our children were little, they used to sledge on that land,' the woman says.

The boys look at each other.

One hundred dollars is a great start for G.E.T.T.H.E.M.

Matthew nods. 'We'll do it.'

'Great.' She smiles. 'Now if only I can get the smell out of my car. I don't suppose that you would be interested in doing that, would you?'

Matthew gets a brainstorm. 'You would just pay the regular price to get your car done, right?'

She nods. 'That cheque is really all that we can afford.'

Matthew grins as he thinks about how bad the car smells.

'Some of the other kids in our class are doing a car wash. You should just pay them the regular price that they are asking to wash cars. Here's the address of where to go.' Matthew writes Vanessa's address on a piece of paper, since that's where the girls are having their car wash. 'By the time you get your car clean, we'll have Puppy here smelling as good as new.'

'Do you promise to take good care of my dog while I'm gone?' The woman looks at the boys.

Brian steps forward. 'I promise. My parents are inside, and once we get this dog cleaned up, I'll put it in my sister's room for safe keeping. I promise.'

As the woman drives off, the boys smile as they think of the girls having to clean that car and getting very little money for it.

And then they hold their noses and get to work.

Chapter 12

'You dweeble. You double dweeble. You dirty double-crossing double dweeble.' Jil! Hudson stands in front of Matthew's locker, grinning at him. 'Someday I'll pay you back for what you did. Do you have any idea how smelly that station wagon you sent over was?'

Matthew nods. 'You should have smelled the dog.'

'Our team was trying to figure out how to get even. We were hoping that someone brought the skunk or a boy-eating piranha to be washed.' Jil! shakes her head. 'Vanessa's mom contributed two cans of air freshener to the cause.'

'We put perfume on the dog. When the lady picked him up, she said that he smelled like Eau de Bow Wow, or something like that,' Matthew says. 'How many cars did you wash?'

'All of our parents' cars and about eight others. Your mother brought her station wagon over. Boy, does she have a lot of fun stuff in there for her business. I asked her if I could have a job as soon as I'm old enough. I'd love to deliver balloons dressed as a chicken, or we could both deliver balloons. I could be Dweebledee and you could be Tweebledum.' Jil! imagines what they would look like in those costumes and who they would be delivering balloons and a message to, dressed like that.

Matthew has several thoughts. One is how come his mother helped the girls earn money when she knows the two teams are competing. He is glad that he didn't have to wash the car. And he wonders why he likes talking to Jil! so much and when she got cute and when he started to notice that she was so cute. This last thought is a very puzzling development to Matthew Martin.

'How many animals did you wash? Enquiring minds want to know.' Jil! asks.

Matthew counts on his fingers. 'We had seven dogs, two cats . . . boy, do they scratch . . . and some lady brought her two-year-old kid who refuses to take a bath. Even she called him El Stinko.'

Jil! giggles. 'What did you do with El Stinko?'

'We told him that he was going to be able to play with "the big boys" and that we were playing "water wrestle with the halloween football," which we made up but which worked. Then we ran after him, watered him down with the hose, soaped him up, rinsed him off, and dried him with Mrs Bruno's hair dryer. He loved it. His mother asked us if we'd do it every night.'

'Tyler told Zoe how much money you made, how much the smelly dog and car lady paid you.' Jil!

makes a face. 'I guess you beat us. But we would have made more if someone hadn't pulled down some of our posters.'

Matthew is surprised. He didn't know about that happening.

Jil! continues, 'You didn't do that, did you? Vanessa said it was probably you, but I said I didn't think you would do anything like that.'

Matthew shakes his head no.

He wouldn't do anything like that, although he and the other boys did ask their parents not to take their cars over to the girls' car wash. He did that after he heard that the girls asked their parents not to take pets to the animal wash.

Matthew is kind of glad that his mother didn't listen, because something about what is going on doesn't seem right to him.

Even though he wants to win, he wants to make money for the conservancy more. Something definitely doesn't seem right.

Vanessa walks over and looks at Jil!. 'Traitor. You're talking to the enemy.'

Jil! looks first at Vanessa, then at Matthew, then over at Cathy Atwood, who isn't in any group, because her father is also trying to buy the land and Cathy didn't think she should work against him. Cathy is standing alone by her locker, looking very unhappy.

Jil! looks at Vanessa. 'I'll talk to anybody I want to.'

Vanessa says the one thing she thinks is going to make Matthew feel bad: 'Aren't you two getting lovey-dovey? I guess you're going to be the next class couple.'

Matthew looks at Jil!, who is blushing a little but looking at Vanessa as if she's slug slime.

He can feel that he is also turning a little red too. 'That's impossible, because I heard that you and King Kong are going to be the next class couple.'

Vanessa opens her mouth to say something else that is nasty.

Before she has a chance, Matthew says, 'I've had it, no more. This is dumb. We're supposed to be working to buy the land. We all would have made more money this weekend if we didn't tell people not to go to the other group. I didn't tear down your dumb posters, but if one of our guys did, that was wrong. I know you don't like me. Well, I don't like you either. But I think everyone should work together. Vanessa, we'll just work together apart.'

Vanessa says, 'You can't make us all work together. You're just trying to break up G.E.T.H.I.M.'

Matthew says something that is always said to him, that he never expected to be saying to anyone else. 'You are *so* immature.'

Jil! adds, 'And I have a feeling that we're not the only people who think we should all work together.'

Vanessa, who is not sure of what to say, says the one thing that she can think of. 'Well, I hope that the two of you are very happy together.' And stomps off.

'Quadruple dweeble.' Jil! looks at her and then

turns to Matthew. 'Look, just because she said all of that stuff doesn't mean that you have to rush out and buy me an engagement ring or anything.'

'What a relief,' Matthew kids.

'That doesn't mean that you can't call me sometimes.' Jil! is feeling very bold.

'What should I call you?' Matthew teases.

Jil! feels a little weird because she was so bold and that Matthew is probably never going to want to talk to her again, at least not without teasing her.

Matthew wonders for a minute if this is what his mother would call 'adolescence onset' and looks at Jil! 'Actually, I'd kind of like to call you and stuff.'

The bell rings.

They smile at each other.

As they walk to class, Matthew says, 'Let's talk to the two groups and plan a project together.'

Jil! nods. 'And let's figure out what we can do so that Cathy doesn't feel so bad about not being included.'

Matthew thinks, Maybe 'adolescence onset' is not going to be such a terrible thing.

Then he has an awful thought.

What if he starts acting like Amanda?

Nah!

Chapter 13

'Show time.' Mrs Stanton claps her hands. 'Let's get this show on the road.'

Mrs Stanton always says that when the class is going to start something that she considers exciting.

However, she never says that before a spelling, maths, or grammar test.

Mrs Stanton smiles at the class. 'You know that because of what's been happening with the property next door to the school, I've decided that we should study our own history, to understand why people feel the way they do about land . . . why some people want to preserve it and why others want to see the town grow and change. This will help you to make your own decisions. Now, who has some interesting facts about Califon? You may use your notes.'

Notebooks are taken out and hands are raised.

'Ow. Ow. Ow.' Jil! always makes that noise when she wants to be called on.

Mrs Stanton nods.

Jil! takes a very deep breath and begins. 'Califon is just a little more than two square miles. . . . It's in

Hunterton County, New Jersey, and in 1850 it was originally named California.'

She pauses to take a breath.

Mrs Stanton immediately says, 'Does anyone know why it was named California?'

'My turn,' Jessica calls out.

Once Jil! starts, it's hard for anyone else to get in a word, so everyone tries to act quickly.

Mrs Stanton nods. 'Go on.'

'It was named California because some guy named Jacob Neighbor was important in town, and that's where he came from,' Jessica says. 'It's funny. If he had come from Arizona, maybe we'd be living in a place called Arizon or something.'

'My turn,' Billy Kellerman says. 'Once there was an area called Peggy's Puddle. . . . And speaking of water, sometime in the early 1930s there was a chance that a dam was going to be built and there would be no more Califon.'

'That would be a dam shame,' Matthew says.

Jil! grins at him.

Vanessa scowls.

Mrs Stanton says, 'Matthew.'

'I didn't say anything wrong.' He grins.

'Three facts, please,' his teacher says.

Vanessa hopes that he can't think of three facts and that everyone will think he's a doofus.

Matthew thinks about his research and the facts that he liked best. Actually the dam one was his favourite, but he is sure that he can come up with others.

'I'm waiting,' Mrs Stanton says.

Matthew nods. 'Three facts. In 1903 indoor plumbing began. Everyone was very happy about that. In 1918 Califon Electric Light and Power Company brought electricity to the town.'

'How did they use their hair dryers before that?' Chloe shows concern for the early Califon residents.

Matthew continues, 'The first telephones, nine of them, came in 1903. They had to use switchboards. That means that all calls went to somewhere else first and then to the house. And everyone had party lines.'

'Party,' Mark yells out.

Mrs Stanton says, 'Party lines means that you have to share them and that each house has a specific sound of ringing.'

'And other people can listen in?' Zoe looks at Tyler.

Mrs Stanton says, 'They weren't supposed to.'

'What fun,' Ryma, who loves gossip, says.

'Back in the old days, did you have party lines?' Sarah asks.

'Yes.' Mrs Stanton remembers. 'When I was little, there was a changeover to dial.'

'Wow. Ancient history,' Chloe gasps.

'Not exactly as far back as Cleopatra,' Mrs Stanton reminds them. 'I'm not that old.'

Pablo Martinez, who is mathematically inclined, calculates that Mrs Stanton is about four times as old as they are, not all of them together but each of them. He also figures that in dog years Mrs Stanton would be about three hundred and eight years old.

To him that seems like ancient history for children and animals. He does not, however, choose to mention this to Mrs Stanton.

Somewhere in the back of Mrs Stanton's head she is trying to remember what she thought was old age when she was eleven or twelve.

The thought is depressing her just a little.

Matthew, however, is feeling great that he was able to give three facts.

He looks over at Jil!, who grins and mouths the words, 'My hero.'

He does not look over at Vanessa, who is annoyed because he used the facts that she remembered.

'Anything else you want to share?' Mrs Stanton asks.

Lizzie calls out, 'I have a great true story. My parents told it to us at dinner last night. It's about "The Great Califon Duck Roundup." What happened was that shortly after one of the mayors got into office, he decided that there were too many ducks in Califon River and that they were going to starve to death. So he decided that as a good deed, he would have "The Great Califon Duck Roundup." He had the chief of police take him out on the river in a rowing boat. Then he threw bread out of the boat so that the ducks would follow him. Then he was going to beach the boat and throw some bread into a caged-in area. The ducks were expected to follow and get captured. Then the ducks would be sent off to other places. The ducks followed him but they wouldn't go into the cage.

They went back into the water.'

Cathy Atwood adds, 'My mother says that her family had a favourite duck so they put food colouring on that duck so that if it got captured, they could come get it.'

'My dad told me that the mayor said that if it didn't work, he would become a lame duck mayor,' Lizzie says. 'My mom laughed, but I don't get it.'

'It's not nice to make fun of ducks with orthopaedic problems.' Sarah makes a face.

Mrs Stanton explains that *lame duck* in government means that the official will not be serving the next term.

Sarah feels much better.

Everyone continues to talk about the town and how some of them have always lived there and how some have just been living there for a short time.

Then they all begin to talk about where all of their families came from and how they feel about Mrs Nichols's land.

Everyone is beginning to realize about how history isn't just something to study, that they all have their own histories of who they are and where their families have lived.

'Okay,' Mrs Stanton claps her hands. 'We've got the show on the road.'

Everyone is feeling very pleased.

'Homework tonight,' she informs them.

Everyone is not so pleased.

'I want everyone to write a paper entitled "What Califon Means to me."' Mrs Stanton assigns the work. 'You may take out your notebooks and start now.'

'How long does it have to be?'

'Does spelling count?'

Mrs Stanton ignores the questions.

As everyone begins, Matthew thinks about all the things that always have been important to him and about the things that are becoming important to him now. It's as if now he's old enough to begin writing 'The Matthew Martin Story.'

He looks at Jil! and thinks that maybe he would like to be at least a chapter in any book she'd write. He looks at Vanessa and figures any book that she would write would sit in a library and collect mould. He looks around the room and realizes that there are a lot of people in the room whose story he would really like to read.

WHAT CALIFON

MEANS TO ME

by Matthew Martin

I'm just a kid and normally I don't think a lot about this subject. (Except when my teacher makes me - just kidding).

I like living in Califon.

For one thing it's an easy place to spell. I would be in deep trouble if I lived in a place like Albakirkee, New Mexico, or Metuchen, New Jersey. (My parents' friends live there and personally I think it should be spelled Mitt-Touch-In.) Another town that I would have trouble living in is Piscataway, New Jersey. (I'm not even going to tell you how I think that town should be spelled.)

Another thing I like is that you get to know people in your class. (That's good except for one person and I'm not going to mention her name because to quote my teacher, you, Mrs Stanton, 'If you can't say something nice about someone, you shouldn't say anything at all.' So I won't even mention the V.S.'s name.) It's not like in some places, where there are so many kids, you never know who they are. I bet I can tell you the name of every kid in the whole school, even the kindergarten babies.

I also like that everything I need is easy to get to by bike, sweet shops, a bagel place, a sub shop, not where you go to get replacements for sick teachers but really good sandwiches, not the kind that my mother makes. There's not one sprout in any sandwich they sell.

Another good thing is that you can ride a bike just about anywhere. Someday I hope to be riding a Porsche or a Lamborgeknee, but for now Califon is a good place to ride a bike. The busiest street is Main Street and the most you ever have to wait there is two minutes and that's during rush hour. (Maybe they should call it rush minute, or something.) Also, if you get tired of riding a bike and want to sit and rest, there are a lot of trees with a lot of shade. And most people don't chase you away.

A person who really never chases you away is Mrs Nichols. I never used to think about it much because she was always just there (except for when she took her big trip, but I always knew that she was coming back). Anyway, going to visit her has always been fun - the sledging, the skating, the things she gives us to eat. Anyway, I hope that Mrs Nichols and her property are not going to be 'Past History,' that they will still be 'Current events.' My parents and I were talking about all of this last night and they say that it's important not just to conserve the land but to help keep old people as part of our lives. I hope that they can do something. Mrs Nichols has always been a part of my life. There's another thing about her. At Halloween she gives out the best sweets, not the dinky little candy bars made especially for trick-or-treating but the regular ones that you can buy all year round. I don't want you to think I just like her because of the junk food. I really do like her for a lot of reasons, but

I don't want to sound too mushy.

Speaking of Halloween, it's a good time in Califon. Lots of sweets are given out, and the only real danger is having to bob for apples and knowing that Vanessa Singer drools into the water.

Any small crime in Califon is a headline story, so it's really a pretty safe place to live.

My older sister, Amanda, is always saying that she'd like to live somewhere bigger with more stuff to do. Personally I hope that she moves to somewhere bigger too. Alone.

I just thought of something else. Since the school goes from kindergarten to eighth grade, I really know my way around and don't worry about getting lost.

My parents say that they like living here for lots of grown-up reasons. (My mother grew up here and then went away to college and met my father, who grew up in New York City. They lived in New York for a while and then moved here and, as my father says, 'had kids and crabgrass.') I could tell you what they say, but then the homework assignment would have been 'What Califon Means to My Parents.' Maybe on 'Back-to-School Night' you could make them right. Don't worry. They can spell.

To sum all this, I like living here.

THE END

P.S. I spell-checked this on my computer, so my spelling should be better.

P.P.S. I hope that I've written enough for this homework assignment.

Chapter 15

'Matthew, we're here to collect the money.' Lizzie holds out her hand. 'Cough it up.'

There's no way to escape.

Lizzie has Matthew backed up to the wall by the water fountain. Sarah Montgomery and Chloe Fulton are on either side of him.

'Let's make a deal,' Matthew bargains. 'Tomorrow I'll pay double.'

'No dice, Matt.' Lizzie shakes her head.

'Matthew. Not Matt. I like to be called Matthew.' He tries to change the subject. 'Just because you like to have a nickname doesn't mean I do.'

Lizzie shakes her head. 'I know that you like to be called Matthew. That's why I called you Matt. I'm going to do it every time you don't pay up.'

'Just leave me money for one chocolate bar a week,' Matthew pleads. 'I know that we all promised to give up what we spend on sweets each week to the conservancy, but the rest of you have parents who let you have sweets at home. You know that my mom doesn't, and even my dad is pledging the money he usually spends on junk food to the conservancy.'

'That's tough.' Sarah sounds sympathetic. 'Even my horse gets a sugar cube sometimes. I'll bring you something from home tomorrow.'

'Fork it over, or they'll be dragging Califon River for your carcass.' Lizzie has been watching a lot of old gangster movies in order to perfect her collection techniques. 'I haven't got all day. I have to get the money from the rest of the kids.'

Matthew reaches into his pocket, pulls out the money and thinks, Good-bye, M & M's.

He also thinks about how he's been managing to survive without the sweets, that the time that he's been spending with Jil! and his other friends working on the project has kept him really busy and not craving so much junk food.

Still, a couple of M's for old time's sake would not be a bad idea, Matthew thinks.

Lizzie puts the money in an old Garfield lunch box, that she stopped using in the third grade.

The box is filled with change.

'What happens if the conservancy can't raise all the money?' Matthew wonders.

Lizzie has the answer. 'If the conservancy doesn't make enough money to buy the property, the cheques will be returned. The cash that we've all collected from the walkathons, the readathons, the bake sales, auction, and sweets give-up . . . that will go into starting a fund to build a new playground.'

The end-of-school bell rings.

'Drats. We're running late.' Lizzie rushes off to collect more money.

As Chloe leaves, she says, 'Don't forget. We have to get the computer illustrations ready for the cookbook.'

Matthew nods, remembering that the cookbook meeting is going to be held at his house tonight since the computer being used is there.

The cookbook is the sixth grade's special project to earn money for the conservancy.

Matthew rushes to his locker, opens it, and throws his stuff on the bottom.

Actually his stuff goes on top of what is already on the bottom of his locker; more school books, four overdue library books, a nerf ball, a New York Yankees baseball cap, two sweatshirts, a broken pair of sunglasses, and two non-matching gloves.

It's a good thing that his mother never sees his locker or she'd again threaten to call the Board of Health.

The dreaded after-school hunger pangs strike, and Matthew searches the top shelf for any junk food that might have been left there.

No luck.

All he can find is old granola bars, shrivelled-up cinnamon-apple chunks, and carob balls with fluff on them.

There is definitely 'a fungus among us,' thinks Matthew as he debates throwing the food out or putting it in Vanessa Singer's lunch some day.

While he is debating, he hears a sound that is a little like an answering machine.

It's coming from a locker, which Matthew finds a

little strange, since he didn't think that the phone company had started installing phones in lockers.

Matthew looks to his right. The only person there is a fourth-grader who has decided to see if he can fit into his locker.

He looks to the left.

The sound is coming from Zoe's locker.

Zoe and Chloe are standing by the locker, looking at a piece of equipment that Zoe has placed on the inside of the door.

Matthew eavesdrops as Zoe explains.

'My mother gave this to me. See, this is a machine that you hook up inside the locker. It comes with three whistles, which you give out to three friends. They come up to the locker and whistle. That activates the tape recorder and they leave a message for me, not more than twenty seconds' worth, and then I can hear the message when I come back to the locker.'

This information explains why Matthew had seen Tyler blowing kisses into her locker earlier in the day.

Matthew is relieved to know that Tyler has not developed a sudden attraction for lockers.

Zoe continues, 'Three whistles are not really enough. I ordered six more.'

Matthew wants to go over and ask Zoe why she bothers having the machine when anyone who wants to leave her a message can just tell her in class.

He decides not to go over, because then they'll

know that he's eavesdropping.

Pretending to search the bottom of his locker, he tries to figure out how to invent something that will sound like one of her whistles so that he can leave her messages that will make her think that her locker has been haunted.

Joshua comes over. 'We have that dumb cookbook meeting. How did we get involved in doing that so we can't go over to my house and play Nintendo tonight?'

He dribbles an imaginary basketball, which he then throws to Brian.

Matthew holds his arms together as Brian dribbles the imaginary ball up to him, dunks it in, and yells, 'Two points.'

Joshua repeats, 'So how did we get involved in this stupid cookbook thing?'

'Because we get to eat the samples that people send over,' Matthew reminds him. 'And I get to do some of the computer stuff. You know I like doing that.'

'And Jil! is the editor, and you know how Matthew feels about that,' Brian teases.

Joshua crosses his arms in front of himself and turns his back to the boys.

From the back it looks like Joshua is kissing someone, especially since he keeps moving his arms up and down and saying, 'Oh, Matthew. . . . Oh, Jil!'

Brian starts making kissing sounds on the back of his hand.

Matthew remembers the 'good old days,' when he used to act immature like that.

He forgets that the good old days were less than a month ago.

Chapter 16

Amanda rushes into the rec room.

Her hand covers her left eye. 'I need your help. I really need your help.'

'If it's something medical, you'd better get Mom or Dad. They're in the dining room holding a conservancy meeting,' Matthew says nervously.

'No. I don't want them to know. I dropped one of my contact lenses on my bedroom floor and I need help finding it.' Amanda is almost breathless. 'Honey, baby. Please help.'

'Everyone's coming here for the cookbook meeting.' Matthew continues doing a computer illustration. 'I don't have time. How come you always say stuff like "Make like a tree and leave" and then, when you want something, it's "honey baby"?'

Amanda knows that he is right.

She also knows that her parents are going to be *very* angry if she's lost another lens.

After the third one went down the sink, they told her that they wouldn't claim another one on the insurance or they might lose the policy and that she would have to buy the next one herself.

Joshua walks into the recreation room, sits down, and listens.

Amanda begs again. 'Please, Matthew. I dropped the lens when I rubbed my eye, and now it's somewhere on the carpet and I can't find it. And now I'm getting dizzy from using just one eye.'

'Getting dizzy!' Matthew looks up from the picture he is doing of Mrs Stanton's spaghetti recipe. 'You normally are dizzy.'

Amanda gets ready to yell, until she remembers that she wants something from Matthew. 'Please. Look. This is going to cost me a lot of money and I don't have a lot right now. I took what I've been saving and contributed it to the conservancy.'

Matthew stares at her. 'You're not just saying that?'

'Honest.' Amanda raises her hand, the one that is not covering her eye, and swears, 'I promise.'

Pushing the keys to make sure to save the computer illustration, Matthew says, 'Oh, okay. But just remember . . . this tree is not planning on leaving any time soon, and I don't want to be told to go any more. I have just as much right to be here as you do.'

Amanda has no choice but to nod.

'When the rest of the kids get here, you can feed them some of the junk in the refrigerator. My dad and I went shopping, so don't worry,' Matthew tells Joshua. 'I'll help Cyclops, the one-eyed monster, and then be back.'

As Amanda and Matthew head out of the room,

Matthew says, 'Remember the other day when I was sick and got to stay home from school?'

Amanda remembers.

She definitely remembers.

That was the day she came home from school, opened her private diary, which she kept hidden under her mattress, and found out that Matthew had written comments in the margins.

So Amanda does remember but decides that now is not the time to start screaming again.

Matthew continues. 'Well, there was this television show that had this helpful-hints person on . . . and the helpful hint for that day was how to find contact lenses, the hard kind, on rugs.'

'How come you didn't tell me about it?' Amanda asks.

'You were too busy trying to kill me.' Matthew is sure that his sister was most upset because on the page in her diary where she gave grades to the rear ends of the boys in her class, he wrote, 'BUTT BRAIN.'

Amanda is careful not to start yelling again, concentrating instead on how happy she will be if they can find the contact lens.

'Take off your shoes,' she warns him. 'You might break the lens if you step on it with your shoe. I'll try using the torch again to look, to see if the light shows where it is and you tell me about the helpful hint.'

Matthew says, 'Get the vacuum cleaner.'

'You're crazy.' Amanda gasps.

Matthew glares.

'Sorry.' Amanda speaks softly.

'And a pair of tights.' Matthew can hear a car pull up in the driveway and wonders if everyone is downstairs waiting for him, and whether they are eating up all the junk food before he returns.

She races to get the vacuum cleaner and then hands him the tights.

'Gross,' he says holding them. 'Don't you feel like you've been tied in rubber bands when you wear this?'

'They're Mom's support tights. Don't tell her I took them.' Amanda giggles. 'I'm down to my last pair of regular stockings and didn't want to take a chance on ripping them.'

Matthew takes the tights, sticks the vacuum cleaner hose on the inside part of the leg and turns on the vacuum.

'We put this on the rug where you think that you dropped the lens and it'll pick it up without breaking the lens. The tights act like a screen.' Matthew is very proud of himself. He knew that watching that part of the show would come in handy some day, especially with 'lose-a-lens-a-day Amanda' as sister.

Matthew carefully puts the vacuum/tights nozzle near the carpet where Amanda is pointing.

'I think we caught a spider.' Matthew looks at what he has picked up.

'Yuck,' Amanda makes a face and then grins. 'That's my missing false eyelash.'

It's Matthew's turn to go 'Yuck.'

Matthew points the nozzle down again and then

looks at what he has picked up. 'BINGO. One contact lens found.'

Amanda checks and makes sure that it is in good shape. 'Oh, thank you. Thank you. Thank you.'

She goes over to the cleaning solution to get all the carpet fuzz off the lens.

Just as she says, 'Thank you,' Matthew goes 'Faster than a speeding bullet, more powerful than a locomotive, able to leap tall buildings in a single bound, Supermatthew saves the day and returns to the waiting company.'

As he heads out of the room pretending to fly, Amanda admits to herself that there are moments when she actually likes her younger brother.

Then she looks down at her marked-up diary and admits to herself that there are many moments when she doesn't.

Chapter 17

Matthew rushes down the steps and flies into the recreation room.

Everyone is there already and Jil! is leading the meeting. She grins at Matthew and then says, 'Attention, everyone. It's time for the reports. Let's do those quickly so that we can get on to the important stuff, the after-the-reports party.'

Katie raises her hand. 'We have sent out one hundred letters to famous people and are waiting to hear from them.'

'I asked all of the actors for their favourite recipes, and if they were in a television series, I asked them to let me know if there was a part for me. I included my picture,' Jessica informs them.

Mark wishes he had thought of asking the Knicks for an autographed basketball instead of just dumb recipes.

'Cathy. How about your report?' Jil! asks her assistant editor.

Some of the kids think it's a little weird for Cathy to be working on the committee since it is her father who is competing to buy the land, but almost everyone knows how awful she felt not being a part of everything.

Her father was the one who really knew how rotten she felt, so he said that she should find something to do that would benefit everyone, that he would just appreciate it if she didn't say bad things about his work.

Cathy reports, 'We have Mrs Nichols's chocolate chip cookie recipe and she also sent over her recipes for ginger snaps, lasagne, and pudding cake.'

Someone's stomach starts to growl.

Matthew looks around the room, pretending that it's not his. He grabs a strawberry Twizzler.

Cathy continues, 'Matthew's mother gave us her recipe for granola bars.'

Everyone groans, except for Matthew, who starts to make retching sounds.

'Shh. She might hear you,' Jil! whispers. 'We don't want to hurt her feelings.'

Matthew informs her, 'They can't hear from the dining room to here. I've tried to listen when Amanda and Danny are down here making out and I can't hear anything.'

Joshua does his kissing imitation again.

Jessica throws a pretzel at him.

Jil! ignores him and sounds editorial. 'We have to include the recipe. It's not poison, and some people actually like it.'

'Name two,' Matthew wants to know.

'Your mother and my dog.' Joshua starts to laugh.

So does Matthew.

'Speaking of mothers, Joshua, yours gave us a recipe,' Cathy informs him.

Everyone is amazed because Mrs Jackson is a living legend in Califon. She is referred to as the Queen of the Frozen Food Section, the person who hates to cook. Mr Jackson is the great cook in the family. He's already sent over his legendary recipe for Chicken Bombay.

'My mother? A recipe? What did she do? Tear off the directions from a beef pot pie?' Joshua can't believe it.

'No,' Cathy informs him. 'It's a recipe for microwave popcorn. It says, 'Put the bag in the oven and nuke it.'

Everybody laughs and then David Cohen says, 'My mother is really weird about the microwave. When she turns it on, she makes everybody leave the room. She thinks that we're going to get zapped by radioactive rays.'

'Why does she use it, then?' Ryma likes things to be logical.

'It's faster.' David shrugs.

'Parents. They're just so weird sometimes.' Jil! giggles, thinking about her own parents, who sometimes like to pretend that they are old-time movie stars Fred Astaire and Ginger Rogers and dance around the middle of streets. 'And sometimes they're not just weird. They're embarrassing.'

Cathy thinks about what she's been going through lately and says, hoping that there will be no comments, 'My dad sent over a recipe for chilli.'

'Chilli. Is he trying to buy that land too? Is the

recipe called Chilli Con Shopping Centre?' Vanessa laughs.

Jil! gasps. 'You are so mean sometimes.'

Vanessa shrugs. 'I just say what I feel.'

'I think that you should say that you feel stupid, then, because you just said something very stupid.' Matthew turns his back on her.

Everyone sits quietly for a minute, not sure of what to say next.

Challenging Vanessa is not always easy, because then she says rotten things to the person who challenges her.

Matthew doesn't care.

He's had to deal with her before, and this time he's not giving in.

He's also going to try very hard not to act like she acts, so he uses the grown-up voice that he has only used when he's kidding around with his parents. 'Psychologists say that people who are mean to other people have major problems and are going to suffer for it the rest of their lives. Probable outcomes of meanness are body parts falling off, oozing sores, and eventually being put in a rubber room. Nine out of ten health care professionals believe this to be true.'

He grins at Vanessa.

Jil! decides to take control of the situation. 'Chloe. Matthew. Why don't you show everyone the computer drawings that you've done for the cookbook.'

While Chloe and Matthew show everyone their artwork, Vanessa sits at her desk looking angry.

Anyone who looks at her would think that she's angry at someone, but the one she is really angry at is herself. She can't figure out why she's always doing things like this and she can't figure out how to stop.

'And this is the illustration for devilled eggs.' Chloe is holding up a piece of paper. 'I figure that it should look like a regular devilled egg with the outside holding the fixed-up yolk. Matthew, however, thinks we should do a devilled egg with horns and a tail, saying "Ha, ha. The yolk is on you."'

A vote is held and Matthew's drawing is selected.

Then someone asks whose recipe it is, and Cathy looks it up. 'It's the minister's wife.'

'Repeat vote.' Jil! calls out.

A vote is reheld, and Matthew's drawing is not selected.

There's a knock on the door.

Everyone looks out.

There's a six-foot-tall pink chicken.

'Come in.' Jil! calls out and starts to giggle.

Matthew knows who it is immediately.

As he tries to sink into the floor, he thinks, How can she do this to me? My own mother.

The six-foot-tall pink chicken is followed by Mickey and Minnie Mouse, Batman, and someone dressed as a Califon duck. The gorilla is also present.

Joshua is laughing hysterically until he notices a ballerina, dressed in a pink tutu with a moustache. It's his father, who is supposed to be home at this very moment writing the Great American Novel.

Joshua's mother is dressed in a chef's costume.

Everyone in costumes is carrying helium balloons.

They start sprinkling confetti around the room.

The sixth-grades have no idea what is going on.

Finally the Califon duck takes off her mask. It's Mrs Stanton.

Mr Jackson takes off his pink mask, which is decorated with feathers. He leaves on the moustache, which is growing on his face.

Batman leaves his mask on because he likes it so much. He speaks first.

Matthew recognizes his father's voice.

Why aren't all of these people out in the grown-up world doing what they are supposed to be doing? Matthew thinks. They're supposed to be upstairs, doing conservancy stuff.

His father explains. 'We've just finished holding the meeting. We've worked out some very important things and wanted to come down here and tell you about it, when we noticed all of these things lying around that my wife uses in her balloon-message delivering business.'

All the kids look at Matthew, who is beginning to think that this is a lot of fun. After all, a lot of fathers dress in three-piece suits. His dad's just happens to include a cape and a mask.

Mr Martin continues, 'We want everyone to know that the conservancy has enough money to buy the land. Part of it is already collected, part is pledged, and then we have estimated how much money we will get from projects like your cookbook. So we can buy the land.'

All the kids start to cheer and applaud, even Cathy, who hopes that her father doesn't find out about her reaction.

Sarah, Ryma, and Patrick do the whistle that they have been practising . . . the one that they are going to use to get cabs when they all grow up and move to New York City.

'Settle down for a minute. I have more good news.' Mr Martin takes a moment to adjust his mask. 'Mrs Nichols is feeling much better. We just used the speaker phone to talk to her.'

Everyone applauds again.

'I'm really going to miss her,' Jill sighs.

Mr Martin holds up his hands for emphasis. 'There is even more good news. Dr Kellerman is going to be able to do a hip replacement on her and thinks that eventually she will be able to walk again and hopefully be self-sufficient. In any case, with the money coming in, Mrs Nichols will be able to have home care. And this is the best news: For as long as she is able to, she will be able to continue to live in her own home.'

More applause.

Mr Martin decides not to explain all the things that have been worked out, how Mrs Nichols wants to will everything to the town for the children's use when she dies, how, since she had no family, he has promised to be her guardian if she ever gets very old and frail and can't take care of herself. He just wants everyone to know the really wonderful news for now.

The land is saved.

Mrs Nichols has a home.

Everyone runs around the room giving high fives.

Joshua looks at his father and thinks about how ridiculous it is for an overweight middle-aged man in a pink tutu and a moustache to be jumping up and down giving high fives.

Matthew looks over at his father and listens to what Mr Martin is saying to his mother. 'Life's not always easy . . . or fair . . . and it certainly doesn't always end with "and they lived happily ever after." I'm glad that this time things turned out so well.'

And then Matthew watches Batman kiss the six-foot-tall pink chicken.

He watches as Mrs Stanton, dressed as the Califon duck, stands over Zoe and Tyler, who will use any excuse to kiss.

Mrs Stanton taps them on their shoulders and says, 'Cool it, kids.'

Matthew wonders if Mrs Stanton will do the same thing to his parents.

Then he turns to Jil!

'We did it! We all did it.' She reaches out and hugs him.

Soon everyone is hugging everyone else.

Finally, when everything settles down, Matthew looks at everyone and says, 'So when do we start working on getting the playground built?'

And so it ends and begins again.

All Pan books are available at your local bookshop or newsagent, or can be ordered direct from the publisher. Indicate the number of copies required and fill in the form below.

Send to: Pan C. S. Dept
              Macmillan Distribution Ltd
              Houndmills Basingstoke RG21 2XS

or phone: 0256 29242, quoting title, author and Credit Card number.

Please enclose a remittance* to the value of the cover price plus £1.00 for the first book plus 50p per copy for each additional book ordered.

*Payment may be made in sterling by UK personal cheque, postal order, sterling draft or international money order, made payable to Pan Books Ltd.

Alternatively by Barclaycard/Access/Amex/Diners

Card No. | | | | | | | | | | | | | | | | | | |

Expiry Date | | | | | | |

_____

Signature: `

Applicable only in the UK and BFPO addresses

While every effort is made to keep prices low, it is sometimes necessary to increase prices at short notice. Pan Books reserve the right to show on covers and charge new retail prices which may differ from those advertised in the text or elsewhere.

NAME AND ADDRESS IN BLOCK LETTERS PLEASE:

....

Name_____

Address_____

_____

_____

_____

6/92